MAURICE

Queer Film Classics
Edited by Matthew Hays and Thomas Waugh

The enduring commercial success of LGBTQ2I films over recent generations offers proof of widespread interest in queer film within both pop culture and academia. Not only are recent works riding the wave of the new maturity of queer film culture, but a century of queer and proto-queer classics are in busy circulation thanks to a burgeoning online queer cinephile culture and have been brought back to life by omnipresent festivals and revivals. Meditations on individual films from queer perspectives are particularly urgent, unlocking new understandings of political as well as aesthetic and personal concerns.

Queer Film Classics at McGill-Queen's University Press emphasizes good writing, rigorous but accessible scholarship, and personal, reflective thinking about the significance of each film – writing that is true to the film, original, and enlightening and enjoyable for film buffs, scholars, and students alike. Books in the series are short – roughly 40,000 words – but well illustrated and allow for considerable depth. Exploring historical, authorial, and production contexts and drawing on filmic analysis, these open-ended essays also develop the author's personal interests or a subjective reading of the work's sexual identity discourses or reception. The series aims to meet the diversity, quality, and originality of classics in the queer film canon, broadly conceived, with equally compelling writing and critical insight. Books in the series have much to teach us, not only about the art of film but about the queer ways in which films can transmit our meanings, our stories, and our dreams.

MAURICE

David Greven

McGill-Queen's University Press

Montreal & Kingston | London | Chicago

© McGill-Queen's University Press 2023

ISBN 978-0-2280-1877-3 (cloth)
ISBN 978-0-2280-1878-0 (paper)
ISBN 978-0-2280-1917-6 (ePDF)
ISBN 978-0-2280-1918-3 (ePUB)

Legal deposit third quarter 2023
Bibliothèque nationale du Québec

Printed in Canada on acid-free paper that is 100% ancient forest free
(100% post-consumer recycled), processed chlorine free

Library and Archives Canada Cataloguing in Publication

Title: Maurice / David Greven.
Names: Greven, David, author.
Series: Queer film classics.
Description: Series statement: Queer film classics | Includes bibliograph-
    ical references and index.
Identifiers: Canadiana (print) 20230191533 | Canadiana (ebook)
    20230191576 | ISBN 9780228018773 (hardcover) | ISBN 9780228018780
    (softcover) | ISBN 9780228019176 (PDF) | ISBN 9780228019183 (EPUB)
Subjects: LCSH: Maurice (Motion picture) | LCSH: Ivory, James—Criti-
    cism and interpretation. | LCSH: Homosexuality in motion pictures. |
    LCSH: Gay men in motion pictures. | LCSH: Motion pictures—Great
    Britain—History.
Classification: LCC PN1997.M38 G74 2023 | DDC 791.43/72—dc23

Contents

Preface

Maurice, *C'est Moi*

I first saw the Merchant Ivory film *Maurice* in 1987, the year of its initial release.
Having moved back to New York City to start college (my parents had fled
the city in the 1970s for the beckoning suburban allure of New Jersey), I was
rediscovering the city. It rained all afternoon the day I ventured from Inwood
(past Washington Heights, the last stop in Manhattan) to 59th Street, where
the Paris Theater was showing the film. One of the lenses of my glasses had
been threatening to free itself from the frame, and it did so as I walked the
rain-soaked blocks from the train station to the theatre. I bent down and re-
trieved the lens and put it back inside the frame, where it remained, however
precariously. This moment preceding my experience of seeing the film –
buying the ticket, walking into the theatre where adult and sophisticated (and
… gay?) moviegoers milled about – always seems so inescapably allegorical.
Redolent of my excitement and deep nervousness, my vulnerability but also
ability to keep going – not to lose sight of my goal or my desire.

While out to myself, I was thoroughly closeted to family, friends, the outside
world. Hence my excitement and trepidation at the thought of being in a theatre full of actual gays, those exotic creatures I counted myself among yet felt
unable to join. The closet leaves one perpetually hungry. Steadfast in my se-
crecy, I surreptitiously imbibed contraband knowledge. I read gay-centric pe-
riodicals like *Village Voice*, which typically included not only articles about

downtown gay life and the looming threat of AIDS but also flesh-baring images of contemporary Adonises (Adonis was the name, indeed, of a gay porn theatre in Times Square); reread books like James Baldwin's 1956 novel *Giovanni's Room* and YA gay classics that got me through adolescence such as *I'll Get There. It Better Be Worth the Trip* (1969) by John Donovan; *Sticks and Stones* (1972) by Lynn Hall; and, less conventionally since they did not contain explicit gay themes, Lois Duncan books like *Killing Mr Griffin* (1978) and *They Never Came Home* (1968). And I had seen Merchant Ivory's film *A Room with a View* (1985) in the theatre and its nude male bathing scene still lurked in my mind and made me know I had to see *Maurice*.

When I made my way to the Paris Theater to see *Maurice*, my triumph was a solitary one. I was alone. No one in my world knew I was gay unless they'd inferred it independently, or I had had a sexual experience with them. So, my aloneness found a complement in Maurice's. Although externally dissimilar, Maurice suffered in ways I responded to intensely; his struggles felt like my own. I remember a palpable, almost tactile thrill when Maurice and the friend he loves, Clive Durham (Hugh Grant), awkwardly but intently and tenderly embrace. I shared Maurice's wound when Clive holds him at bay and rejects him. The bliss Maurice ultimately finds with the gamekeeper Alec Scudder (Rupert Graves) also felt personal.

I mention this feeling of ardent identification in hopes of making a larger point: one need not actually see oneself onscreen to see oneself *in* the work. As the child of immigrant parents, someone of mixed race with a working-class background on both sides, and as an American for that matter, I did not see in Maurice someone who looked or acted in the least as I did. Yet I felt for him intensely and wanted nothing more than his happiness. Alec's seduction of Maurice promised a kind of relief for me too, or so I hoped.

Thus although the rise of identity-politics work has quite rightly sought authentic representation and diversity, it's also important to note that the power of art can speak deeply to us without necessarily resembling us. My mother is from Haiti, and my father is from Argentina, and I have rarely seen

Figure 1
The eloquence of hands. Maurice and Clive intertwine in *Maurice*.

myself on page or screen. Nevertheless, I have greatly benefitted from works of art, from narratives that have captured and expressed, it has sometimes felt, things from my own life. So it was with *Maurice*; I was a solitary wanderer finding refuge.

As a scholar I work in two fields – nineteenth-century American literature, and film studies – and feel kinship with artists like Nathaniel Hawthorne, Herman Melville, Edgar Allan Poe, Henry James, Edith Wharton, and Alfred Hitchcock, and with film genres such as the woman's film and film noir, the upstart visionaries of the New Hollywood and, later, the New Queer Cinema. The social psychiatrist Daryl J. Bem persuasively offered, in a 1996 paper, a theory of homosexual desire – really, of all sexual desire – as having this foundation: "the exotic becomes erotic." This parallels my aesthetic appetites: I want to inhabit lives unlike my own.

Seeing *Maurice* now, I still feel deep kinship with it. It seems to me that the film can scarcely be bettered. James Ivory's direction, the Richard Robbins score, the cinematography by Pierre Lhomme, the screenplay adaptation, and the acting are all glorious. Exquisitely adapted from Forster's equally unsung and eloquent novel, Ivory's film is a vision distinct from Forster's, though there are obvious overlaps.

Almost thirty-five years later, I remain enthralled by *Maurice*, but am less dependent on it to speak for me. Indeed, I feel, to a certain extent, that I must speak for it. *Maurice*, like much of Merchant Ivory's work, has not been treated fairly or generously by critics, including queer theorists who maintain that such works desexualize and distort homosexuality. In the last section, I will address *Maurice*'s reception, in its day and in the realm of queer theory.

Ultimately, *Maurice* is as much about loneliness and isolation as it is about the closet and queer desire. As such, it has overlaps with works such as Hitchcock's great *Marnie* (1964) and one of the least discussed great queer films, *The Delta* (1997), directed by Ira Sachs. Imagine if Alec Scudder were nonwhite and could not achieve romantic bliss with Maurice. *The Delta* gives us this story with harrowing results, emphasizing the themes of immigrant isolation and loss and the supremacy of white males in the gay imaginary. Ivory's film, meanwhile, offers critiques of the stifling effects of class bias and the closet, as well as the representation of loneliness and isolation.

In the end, what makes *Maurice* a resonant text for the LGBTQ+ audience is not just its happy ending (albeit less happy than it may appear) but also the fact that its title character is able to jettison the class system and ties that have kept him a sexual and emotional prisoner. That he can feel for others and feel love for Alec gives us hope, in this time when it is most needed, that not only the systems that constrict us but also the people ensnared by these systems and seemingly doomed to perpetuate them are in fact capable of transformation.

Acknowledgments

It has been an indescribable pleasure, and an honour, to work with the team responsible for bringing this book to publication life. First, I want to thank Thomas Waugh and Matthew Hays, who have envisioned, cultivated, and nurtured the Queer Film Classics book series from its inception to its current revived form. No one could possibly ask for more supportive, insightful, patient, and generous editors, and their selfless devotion to this project is both moving and humbling. I thank Jonathan Crago, editor in chief at McGill-Queen's University Press, for being so painstaking and committed and ethical an editor. The entire team at the press is a model of professionalism, sensitivity, and respect for authors. I profusely thank the anonymous readers of this manuscript for their thorough, deeply insightful, and generous feedback. I'm so grateful to you all. My thanks as well to Gary Needham.

I thank the provost and scholars of King's College, Cambridge and the Society of Authors as the E.M. Forster Estate for granting me permission to quote from E.M. Forster's novel *Maurice*.

I thank the entire creative team that falls under the collective title Merchant Ivory, for the pleasure and fulfillment of their cinema over the years, *Maurice* in particular. And, of course, I thank E.M. Forster for his oeuvre, and for *Maurice* especially.

My greatest thanks, as ever, go to my beloved, Alexander Beecroft.

Synopsis

The film opens with the protagonist Maurice Hall – a middle-class English-man – as a schoolboy. He and his classmates take a walk on the beach, led by their schoolmasters. One of them, Mr Ducie, takes Maurice aside and walks with him privately. Sensing that Maurice has no adult males in his life, Ducie gives Maurice a sex education class, drawing images of male and female sexual organs on the sand and explaining reproduction. Looking at the drawings, the adolescent Maurice remarks, "I think I shan't marry," much to Ducie's dis-may. The schoolmaster invites Maurice to dine with Ducie and his wife one day when Maurice has a wife of his own.

We transition to the year 1909. Maurice is a university student at Cam-bridge, taking ancient Greek with the dean. One of his classmates, the flam-boyant Lord Risley, unexpectedly invites Maurice to his rooms that evening. Maurice accepts the invitation; once there, however, he discovers not Risley but instead Clive Durham, who is from an aristocratic family. Maurice and Clive become good friends. Balking at the dean's advice during translation class to "omit the unspeakable vice of the Greeks" (sodomy), Maurice relates the incident to Clive, who gives Maurice a reading list that includes Plato's *Symposium*, an effort to convey homoerotic feeling.

He and Maurice grow closer, including a physical intimacy without sexual contact. Clive confesses to Maurice that he loves him; Maurice panics and pulls away. Clive pulls away much more emphatically. Their tension continues until Maurice convinces Clive that he returns his love. The men take a daytrip and begin to caress one another while lying on the grass. Though they seem on the verge of making love, Clive puts a stop to this, declaring that he believes adding a sexual dimension to their relationship would "bring us down." Their friendship remains close but platonic. Maurice leaves university after refusing to apologize to the dean for cutting class and takes a job as a London stock-broker, like his father.

Risley is arrested for soliciting homosexual sex. He is sentenced to six months of hard labour and his hopes of a political career are shattered. Profoundly affected by Risley's fate, Clive begins to pull away from Maurice and takes a trip alone to Greece. While there he decides that he and Maurice must end their quasi-romantic relationship, and embrace heterosexuality and marriage. After not answering any of Maurice's letters, Clive returns and explains these changes of heart to his friend. Deeply upset and terrified, Maurice demands that Clive remain his secret lover (without sex) and confidant, but Clive refuses. Spurning Maurice's kiss, Clive pushes him away, and their friendship seems to reach an ignominious end, leaving Maurice especially bereft.

Time passes, and Clive contacts Maurice about Clive's impending nuptials to a woman named Anne Woods. Maurice attends their wedding and begins making regular visits to the Durham estate, Pendersleigh. A new character emerges, Alec Scudder, the Durhams' gamekeeper. Though Alec goes out of his way to interact with "Mr Hall," Maurice treats him very much like a servant. Maurice seeks out the services of a conversion-therapy hypnotist, Mr Lasker Jones. Clive and Anne both mistakenly believe that Maurice is in love with and courting a woman.

During one of his visits to Pendersleigh, Maurice is surprised by Alec's sudden appearance in his room. The two men make love, Maurice losing his virginity at last. Alec writes Maurice a letter telling him to go to the boathouse so they can make love one more time before Alec leaves for Buenos Aires, an emigration arranged by his older brother Fred.

After Maurice and Alec have sex, Maurice has a harder time submitting to conversion therapy. Lasker Jones encourages him to repatriate in a country where homosexuality has been decriminalized, such as France or Italy. Maurice shows him the letter that Alec wrote to him, convinced that the gamekeeper is blackmailing him. Alec surprises Maurice at his workplace in London. Still convinced that the gamekeeper is trying to blackmail him, Maurice treats him coldly, and Alec gets angry and begins making threats. The two escape the rain by visiting the British Museum. Oscillating between friendliness and hostility they come across Ducie, who instantly recognizes Maurice. Alec continues to threaten Maurice by telling Ducie, "I've a serious charge to bring against this gentleman," and after the discombobulated Ducie leaves, Maurice and Alec continue to spar. Once outside, however, they become less antagonistic and rediscover their bond. They spend another night together, this time in a London hotel.

In the morning, Maurice encourages Alec not to go to Argentina but to stay in London instead, so that the two can pursue a life together. Alec calls Maurice's advice "bloody rubbish," saying it would "ruin" them both. Maurice later goes to see Alec off, uncomfortably interacting with the Scudder family and Reverend Borenius, who wants to ensure that Alec will continue his Christian training in Argentina. But Alec misses his boat, and Maurice immediately knows why: he has indeed decided to stay with Maurice in England.

Maurice travels to Pendersleigh, and before seeking out Alec he talks with Clive. Clive still believes that Maurice will marry a woman, but Maurice bluntly tells him that he and Alec have had sex and are in love. After implicitly ending any future contact with Clive, Maurice heads to the boathouse, where he finds Alec waiting for him. The two men kiss passionately and affirm their relationship. The last shots of the film show Clive and Anne embracing on the balcony as Clive remembers images of Maurice from their university days.

Credits

Maurice (1987)
Directed by: James Ivory
Produced by: Ismail Merchant and Paul Bradley
Screenplay by: Kit Hesketh-Harvey and James Ivory
Based on *Maurice* by E.M. Forster

Principal Cast:
James Wilby as Maurice Hall
Hugh Grant as Clive Durham
Rupert Graves as Alec Scudder
Denholm Elliott as Doctor Barry
Simon Callow as Mr Ducie
Billie Whitelaw as Mrs Hall
Barry Foster as Dean Cornwallis
Judy Parfitt as Mrs Durham
Phoebe Nicholls as Anne Durham
Patrick Godfrey as Simcox
Mark Tandy as Risley
Ben Kingsley as Lasker-Jones
Kitty Aldridge as Kitty Hall
Helena Michell as Ada Hall

Catherine Rabett as Pippa Durham
Peter Eyre as Rev. Borenius
Michael Jenn as Archie
Mark Payton as Chapman
Orlando Wells as Young Maurice
Maria Britneva as Mrs Sheepshanks
John Elmes as Hill
Alan Foss as Old Man on Train
Philip Fox as Dr Jowitt
Olwen Griffiths as Mrs Scudder
Christopher Hunter (as Chris Hunter) as Fred Scudder
Alan Whybrow as Mr Scudder
Matthew Sim as Featherstonhaugh
Richard Warner as Judge

Music by: Richard Robbins
Cinematography by: Pierre Lhomme
Edited by: Katherine Wenning
Production Companies: Merchant Ivory Productions and
   Film Four International
Distributed by: Cinecom Pictures (US)
Release date: 5 September 1987 (Venice), 18 September 1987 (US)
Running time: 140 minutes
Country: United Kingdom
Language: English
Budget: £1.58 million
Box office (worldwide gross): $2,642,567

Home Video Releases:
Blu-ray: *Maurice – 30th Anniversary Edition 4K Restoration*
Release date: 5 September 2017

Studio: Cohen Media Group

BLU-RAY BONUS FEATURES:

- James Ivory and Pierre Lhomme on the making of *Maurice*
- New on-stage Q&A w/ James Ivory and Pierre Lhomme moderated by Nicholas Elliott, US correspondent for *Cahiers du Cinema*
- The Story of *Maurice*
- Conversation with the filmmakers
- A director's perspective
- A conversation between James Ivory and Tom McCarthy (director of *Spotlight*)
- Deleted scenes and alternate takes with audio commentary by James Ivory
- Original theatrical trailer
- 2017 Re-release trailer

Blu-Ray and DVD: *Maurice – The Merchant Ivory Collection*

Release date: 24 February 2004

Streaming: *Maurice* is available for streaming on The Criterion Channel.

MAURICE

Chapter 1

A Queer Heritage:
Merchant Ivory and the 1980s

Merchant Ivory – a filmmaking team consisting of the director James Ivory, the producer Ismail Merchant, and the screenwriter Ruth Prawer Jhabvala – reached a commercial and critical turning point with *A Room with a View* (1985), an adaptation of E.M. Forster's 1908 novel. *Room* "remains the high-water mark of Merchant Ivory's commercial success and also served to brand them as the foremost purveyors of what quickly came to be known as 'heritage cinema'" (British Film Institute 2005). *Maurice* (1987) was the film that the team made next.

Having achieved a new level of acclaim and profit with *Room*, the filmmakers might have been expected to give us more of the same, and to some extent they do, returning to Forster. But *Maurice* is far from a romantic comedy. Despite a controversial happy ending, *Maurice* is a brooding and sombre work, and deliberately so. As Ivory remarks, rather than rehiring Tony Pierce-Robert, who shot *Room*, he chose the French cinematographer Pierre Lhomme, perhaps best known for Jean-Pierre Melville's 1969 French Resistance epic *Army of Shadows*, for *Maurice*. "I wanted a cooler look for *Maurice*," remarked Ivory, emphasizing blues, grays, and greens that reflected its sombre themes, rather than *Room*'s sunny Italian vistas.[1]

The box-office-reporting website *Box-Office Mojo* reports stark differences in the earning power of *Room* and *Maurice*. *Room*, according to *Box-Office Mojo*, enjoyed a worldwide gross of $21,041,453, whereas *Maurice*'s worldwide gross was $2,642,567. It grossed $2,484,230 domestically, $50,411 in the UK. Gary Goldstein notes: "Unlike Merchant-Ivory's *A Room with a View*, *Maurice* was not considered a box office hit. This, despite a high-profile release and mostly strong critical support, save the *New Yorker*'s Pauline Kael and, strangely, much of the English press, which, Wilby noted, was 'very mealy-mouthed about it'" (Goldstein 2017).

Nevertheless, *Maurice* did earn Jenny Beavan and John Bright an Oscar nomination for best costume design. And the Venice Film Festival awarded the film best actor (shared by James Wilby and Hugh Grant), a Golden Osella for best score to Richard Robbins, and a Silver Lion for directing to James Ivory (who was also nominated for a Golden Lion).

When Merchant Ivory contacted Kings College, Cambridge, who holds the rights to Forster's work, about adapting Forster's novel *Maurice* (begun in 1913–14, published posthumously in 1971), the trustees initially balked, describing this as a "lesser" work and encouraging Ivory to adapt a different one lest the author's reputation be marred. Moreover Merchant Ivory's long-time screenwriter Ruth Prawer Jhabvala also declined to be involved, ostensibly to work on her novel *Three Continents*. But the real reason, as Ivory reports in his memoir *Solid Ivory*, was because Jhabvala viewed *Maurice* as "sub-Forster" and the potential film as "sub-Ivory." (She nevertheless did make some key contributions behind the scenes, as we'll discuss.) Decades later, Ivory still chafes, saying that he "never forgave" Jhabvala for this "unfair dismissal" (Ivory 2021, 327). *Maurice*'s adaptation was written by Ivory and a newcomer to the team, Kit Hesketh-Harvey. Like Forster Hesketh-Harvey was a graduate of Cambridge University, and at that point also a staff producer for the BBC-TV Music and Arts Department.

Merchant Ivory's cinema has longed served as exhibit A in the trials of the "heritage film," associated with, as Belén Vidal puts it, "a powerful undercurrent of nostalgia for the past conveyed by historical dramas, romantic costume films, and period dramas" (Vidal 2012a, 1). Received opinion can be damaging to the work of serious artists. Merchant Ivory has suffered from

Figure 2
James Ivory at the University of Oregon Cinema Studies Program in 2010.
Photo: Amanda Garcia, Flickr.

these clichéd associations, leaving their works including *Maurice* frequently misunderstood.[2]

This chapter explores three principal topics. First, I offer an overview of Merchant Ivory's oeuvre. Second, I address the question of heritage cinema and join critics such as Richard Dyer and Claire Monk in arguing for its queer possibilities. Third, I situate *Maurice* in its 1980s context, both cinematically and politically. Merchant Ivory films *Maurice* and *The Bostonians* (1984), which thematizes lesbian desire, importantly emerged in an era dominated and inextricably shaped by the reigns of Margaret Thatcher and Ronald Reagan and the ever-increasing devastations of AIDS.

Merchant Ivory Begins

James Ivory burst on the cinematic scene with his documentary *Venice: Themes and Variations* (1957). Born in Berkeley, California, in 1928, Ivory spent his formative years in Oregon and attended the University of Oregon. He first studied architecture, then switched to fine arts, earning his degree in 1951. He then earned his master's degree in cinema at the University of Southern California School of Cinematic Arts, submitting *Venice: Themes and Variations* as his master's thesis. It was shown at the Edinburgh Festival in 1957, and the *New York Times* named *Venice* one of the ten best non-theatrical films of the year, an auspicious beginning.[3]

Ivory's second documentary, *The Sword and the Flute* (1959), focuses on the history of Indian miniature painting after the Moghul invasion. *Sword* was narrated by the actor Saeed Jaffrey, who also narrated Ismail Merchant's first film, the fourteen-minute *Creation of Woman*, a tale inspired by Indian mythology. Jaffrey, an Indian actor based in New York, was married to someone whose own fame was on the verge of exploding: Madhur Jaffrey, an actress and food writer who would eventually star in Merchant Ivory films. (Merchant himself would go on to write acclaimed cookbooks, being by all accounts a marvellous chef.) The Jaffreys extolled Ivory to Merchant, who followed their lead and attended a screening of *The Sword and the Flute* at the Indian Consulate in New York City. By all accounts, Ivory and Merchant immediately hit it off, confirming the Jaffreys' matchmaking hunch.

Ismail Noormohamed Abdul Rehman Merchant was born in Bombay in 1936 to Muslim parents. He took the surname Merchant when in college. Though Muslim, Merchant attended Jesuit as well as Muslim schools in Bombay. Raised Catholic, Ivory has disputed the idea that he had a "religious upbringing" yet admits to having a "somewhat theatrically devout period in seventh grade" (Long 1997, 27). It's hard not to read the shared exposure to Catholicism as a link between the two.

Demonstrating his showmanship early on, Merchant parlayed early success with variety shows into funding to attend classes at New York University. These classes were in business administration, but Merchant's passion was for the arts, especially Western music and films. European cinema fuelled his passionate moviegoing, the films of Ingmar Bergman, Vittorio De Sica, and Federico Fellini especially. He had not seen the great Bengali director Satyajit Ray's films in India, but in New York City he devoured them avidly (Long 1997, 27).

In an early example of his entrepreneurial acumen, Merchant was able to get *The Creation of Woman* shown for the requisite number of days to qualify for an Academy Award nomination, and the film received one, giving a considerable boost to Merchant's budding career. Merchant watched *The Sword and the Flute* in New York and met Ivory before heading to the Cannes Film Festival to screen *The Creation of Woman*.

"I realized that he knew about India not in a dry, academic way," Merchant said of Ivory, "but with understanding – something I have never encountered in an American before or since. What was absolutely extraordinary was his *feeling* for India" (Long 1997, 16). Though this aspect of their relationship

Figure 3
James Ivory, Leela Naidu, Shashi Kapoor, and Ismail Merchant at the premiere of
the first Merchant Ivory film, *The Householder*, 1963. Twitter, @FilmHistoryPic.
twitter.com/filmhistorypic/status/1099934433912729601.

would generally not be made public until after Merchant's death at age sixty-
eight, Ivory and Merchant were lovers and life partners as well as artistic
collaborators.

Upon meeting, Merchant and Ivory immediately attempted to collaborate,
going to India later that year to make a film. The funding fell through, but
another bit of serendipitous fortune occurred when they met Ruth Prawer
Jhabvala, their future screenwriter. The German-born novelist was living in
Delhi at the time. The first Merchant Ivory film was their lovely, melancholy
1963 adaptation of Jhabvala's novel *The Householder*, which she adapted for

Figure 4
The Householder already conveys the team's signature lyrical realism. Photo from
https://www.merchantivory.com/film/thehouseholder.

the screen, commencing an extraordinary collaboration among the three that
would endure for decades. (Ivory has reported that Satyajit Ray reedited the
final cut of the film and has often cited Ray as an influence.)

In a profile of Ruth Prawer Jhabvala in the *New Yorker*, Maya Jasanoff writes,
"There's some poignancy in the fact that Jhabvala, who died in 2013, is best
known today as the third member of the Merchant Ivory team. She considered
'writing film scripts' to be a hobby alongside the real work of prose. In her lifetime, she published twelve novels and eight short-story collections. She excelled
at concealing herself, most famously behind her own name" (Jasanoff 2018).

Jhabvala was born Ruth Prawer in Cologne in 1927. Her family was Jewish, assimilated, and middle-class. Barely escaping Hitler's menace, they fled to England in 1939. Jhabvala's father, distraught at how many of his relatives were killed in the Holocaust, died by suicide in 1948. While studying English literature at Queen Mary College, London in 1949, Ruth met Cyrus Jhabvala, an Indian Parsi architect visiting England. The two fell in love, and married when Cyrus Jhabvala landed an academic job in architecture at Delhi Polytechnic. The couple moved to Delhi, and Jhabvala began writing fiction. A satirist working in the vein of Jane Austen, she wrote stories and novels about the intricacies of Indian society. "Jhabvala's early fiction sauntered into middle-class Hindu households and wryly took the measure of their dramatic capacity," observes Maya Jasanoff. "If Jhabvala has an anthropologist's curiosity about how society functions, she's a decidedly nonparticipant observer; her narrative stance brings together candor and detachment" (Jasanoff 2018). That same quality of detachment links her sensibility to James Ivory's cinema, although a distinctive lyricism informs his work.

Given the forty-year span of their collaboration, Ivory, Merchant, and Jhabvala's output – as well as the seven films Merchant directed himself (2001) – demands a much more expansive treatment than this study by its nature allows. Still, we can roughly organize it into the following periods. The early films largely focus on Indian society and the clash between British and Indian ways of life, such as *The Householder, Shakespeare Wallah* (1965), *The Guru* (1969), *Bombay Talkie* (1970), *Autobiography of a Princess* (1975). The team then made *The Europeans* (1979), adapted from a Henry James novel (one of his rare comic works). This first of their adaptations of James yielded sizable American and international audiences. Their best-known works would follow, in rapid succession: *Heat and Dust* (1983), starring Julie Christie and adapted by Jhabvala from her Booker Prize-winning novel; *The Bostonians* (1984), another adaptation of Henry James, starring Vanessa Redgrave and Christopher Reeve; *A Room with a View* (1986); *Maurice* (1987); *Howards End* (1992), starring Anthony Hopkins, Vanessa Redgrave, and Emma Thompson, who won a Best Actress Oscar; and *The Remains of the Day* (1993), adapted from Kazuo Ishiguro's novel and reuniting Thompson and Hopkins. The films made in these years are generally considered peak Merchant Ivory.

Slaves of New York (1989), based on the novel by Tama Janowitz (who wrote the screen adaptation), with its depiction of downtown grungy-hipster New York City art-world types, presaged the next phase of Merchant Ivory's cinematic output. After 1993, the team sought to diversify, shaking up their brand and binding associations with the heritage film. Films that followed include *Jefferson in Paris* (1995); *Surviving Picasso* (1996); *A Soldier's Daughter Never Cries* (1998); another adaptation of Henry James, *The Golden Bowl* (2001), starring Uma Thurman and Nick Nolte; *Le Divorce* (2003); and the last film that Merchant produced before his death in 2005, *The White Countess* (2005), little discussed but, in my view, a beautiful and singular work that offers a poignant valedictory to the team's films.

Without Merchant as producer, Ivory made *The City of Your Final Destination* (2009). This adaptation of the Peter Cameron novel was to be the last screenplay Jhabvala wrote; she died in 2013, having won Best Adapted Screenplay Oscars twice (for *A Room with a View* and *Howards End*). She remains the only person to have won an Oscar and the Booker Prize for fiction (awarded to her novel *Heat and Dust*, which she adapted for Merchant Ivory).

Ivory has continued to work in the wake of Merchant's death. Most notably, Ivory became the oldest Academy Award winner ever for his screenplay adaptation of André Aciman's novel *Call Me by Your Name*, made into a widely beloved 2017 film by Luca Guadagnino. (In cheeky fashion Ivory wore a black jacket and bowtie with a T-shirt created by artist Andrew Mania that had Timothée Chalamet's face on it.) In the wake of his Oscar win and Merchant's death, Ivory has become much more vocal about Merchant's having been his life partner.

Thomas Waugh, in an unpublished 1987 review collected in his book *The Fruit Machine*, discusses the powerful effect that *Maurice* had on him. I want to underscore a point that Waugh made early on about Merchant Ivory: "let's take the liberty of bestowing on them henceforth the honorary label of 'gay filmmakers': though they've never made a Fassbinder-style big deal about their private lives, the usually reliable *People* magazine's profile of the pair last year made no bones about their long-standing cohabitation" (Waugh 2000, 190).

Despite *People*, many people did not know that Ivory and Merchant were life partners; I certainly didn't when I first saw *Maurice*. In the wake of Merchant's death and his bravura Oscar win, Ivory has made the nature of his relationship with Merchant public. In a now-viral interview in the *Guardian* with Ivory, Ryan Gilbey writes Ivory "is gay. His relationship with his producing partner Ismail Merchant, which began when they met in the early 60s, lasted until, following surgery for abdominal ulcers, Merchant died in 2005 during the filming of *The White Countess*, at the age of 68. Though the pair had been making films for more than four decades – often with their friend and favourite screenwriter, Ruth Prawer Jhabvala, who died in 2013 – any references to their personal life together were only ever made discreetly and euphemistically by the press, if at all." When Gilbey pressed Ivory about the couple's reticence to discuss their relationship, Ivory came as close to calling him "a blasted fool as someone so urbane can." "Well, you just wouldn't," Gilbey spluttered. "That is not something that an Indian Muslim would ever say publicly or in print. Ever! You have to remember that Ismail was an Indian citizen living in Bombay, with a deeply conservative Muslim family there. It's not the sort of thing he was going to broadcast. Since we were so close and lived most of our lives together, I wasn't about to undermine him" (Gilbey 2018). Another important collaborator in the Merchant Ivory film world deserves mention. *The White Countess* would be the last of the team's films scored by Richard Robbins, who died in 2012. His first score was for *The Europeans*, and his partnership with Merchant Ivory thrived thereafter. Robbins and Merchant Ivory's relationship bears a significance, in terms of sustained collaborations between composers and filmmakers, equal to that between Bernard

Herrmann and Alfred Hitchcock, Howard Shore and David Cronenberg, and John Williams and Steven Spielberg.

As one critic puts it, "In Merchant Ivory films, music is often depicted as a liberation from the repressions and social charades that bear down on most of the characters; it provides a secret and dangerous window into one's true passions ... Mr Robbins's lush, mannered scores, however, often reflect the repression rather than the liberation" (Strauss 1996). Another critic describes his contributions this way: "Robbins achieved particular distinction in his music for the three Merchant-Ivory films taken from E.M. Forster novels (*A Room with A View*, 1986, *Maurice*, 1987, and *Howards End*, 1992), as well as in *Remains of the Day* (1993) and *Surviving Picasso* (1996). These reveal a consistent style, in which plaintive melodic fragments are superimposed upon recurring rhythmic and harmonic patterns, often in a neo-Baroque, Impressionist, or Minimalist vein. The music rarely mimics particular screen actions or ties itself thematically to individual characters, but provides moody and shimmering atmosphere (often enhanced by synthesizer tracks)" (Marks 2001).

The *Guardian*'s obituary for Robbins put the matter concisely: "The reason for the endurance of Merchant Ivory Productions was the exceptionally happy balance of similarities and contrasts between its members. Although from a different background, Robbins shared the cultured, cosmopolitan sensibilities of the others, which allowed him to make a significant contribution to the literate, ironic, refined and beautifully designed Merchant Ivory movies" (Bergan 2012). The obituary makes note of the range of Robbins's music: a jazzy foxtrot for *Quartet* (1981), Indian themes in *Heat and Dust*, a percussive soundtrack for *Mr and Mrs Bridge* (1990), a "modern-sounding classicism" for *Jefferson in Paris* (1995), and Richard Straussian tones for *The Golden Bowl*.

Not insignificantly, Robbins was also a gay man, survived by his partner, the artist Michael Schell. Merchant Ivory is often described as a team consisting of a Catholic (Ivory), a Muslim (Merchant), and a Jew (Jhabvala). Another way of thinking about it is that for the portion of the forty-four-year Merchant

Ivory collaboration that included Robbins, it was an intellectually polyamorous relationship among three gay men and a straight woman.

Queering the Heritage Film: Adapting James and Forster

Andrew Higson's 1993 article "Re-presenting the National Past: Nostalgia and Pastiche in the Heritage Film" established the elements typically associated with the heritage film and modelled the negative response to the genre as reactionary and classist, deeply limited and limiting in its presentation of what constitutes Englishness.

Noting the international success of such British films as *Chariots of Fire* (1981) and *Gandhi* (1982), both winners of Best Picture Oscars, Belén Vidal summarizes the term "heritage film": "The heritage film has period settings (typically, Edwardian England or the British Raj), recurrent locations (the English countryside, Oxbridge, colonial India, Italy), slow-paced narratives that enhance character and the authenticity of period detail, and an opulent if static mise-en-scène exhibiting elaborate period costumes, artifacts, properties and heritage sites." Vidal summarizes Higson's views. Heritage films foreground "upper-middle class and aristocratic privilege," which "produces a highly selective vision of Englishness" (Vidal 2012a, 8). Claire Monk observes that the "idea, and critique, of heritage cinema first emerged in Britain in the late 1980s to early 1990s as a deferred response from the academic/intellectual left to certain British period films produced or released since the early 1980s – at the height of Thatcherite Conservatism – and argued to be ideologically complicit with it" (Monk and Sargeant 2002a, 177).

"Quality" is a term of abuse for those who view heritage films negatively. For such critics, these films are "aesthetically conservative; uncinematic in that they favoured a static pictorialism rather than making the fullest use of the moving image; and their claims to 'quality' rested on a second-hand affiliation with 'high' literary and theatrical culture which flattered audiences while appealing to cultural snobberies" (Monk and Sargeant 2002a, 178). Higson has shaped, through his frequent writings on the subject, our general understanding of what is meant by "heritage cinema," especially as associated with British cinema.[4] Yet he has repeatedly qualified and re-examined his earlier positions in several subsequent studies. "My argument in 'Re-presenting the national past' was heavily marked by a very ambivalent response to the films I was discussing," Higson later wrote. He acknowledges that he was first motivated to expose "the conservatism of the heritage industry and of middle-class quality cinema." Yet he also "had to take on board the fact that I also rather enjoyed these films, although I'm not sure I felt that I could admit as much, since this would reveal my own class formation, my own cultural inheritance, my attachment to the wrong sort of cinema for a Film Studies lecturer" (Higson 1997b, 238). He echoes Laura Mulvey's somewhat rueful tone in her essay "Afterthoughts on 'Visual Pleasure and Narrative Cinema'" – a response to her iconic 1975 essay for *Screen* – where she admits to loving classical Hollywood melodrama a great deal more than she'd indicated earlier.

Controversies over the heritage film endure. My focus here, informed by the work of critics such as Richard Dyer and Claire Monk, is on Merchant Ivory films as a *rebuff* to the purported conservatism of the heritage film, particularly in terms of gay and lesbian representation.[5] Merchant Ivory films support Dyer's contention that heritage films put gay men back into history. In a rebuttal to Higson's anti-heritage film views, Claire Monk underscored the resistant nature of Merchant Ivory films, locating their transgressiveness in the depiction of the male body:

In contrast with the model of cinema spectatorship offered by 1970s film theory, in which (in classic narrative films at least) the male gaze is fixed and fixated on the "to-be-looked- at" female form onscreen, the central peculiarity of the best-known heritage films is that it is the men onscreen who are displayed as the spectacle to be looked at, and an audience which (empirical evidence suggests) is largely composed of women and gay men which does the looking. This applies to *A Room With A View* – with its famous male nude bathing scene – as much as to, say, *Maurice*, which explicitly takes "the sexual and emotional education of a homosexual [Edwardian] gentleman" (to borrow a phrase from Mark Sanderson's review of the film for *Time Out* magazine) as its subject. (Monk 1995, 120)

Critics like Michael Williams and Alina Patriche further support the idea of heritage cinema as a place of sexual possibility. Writing affirmatively of *Maurice*, Williams notes that heritage cinema can create spaces for "different readings and even encourage them, particularly with respect to gay sexuality" (Williams 2018, 227). Building on Dyer's essay "Nice Young Men Who Sell Antiques: Gay Men in Heritage Cinema" and Monk's "The British Heritage Film and Its Critics," Patriche elaborates: "Even when the narrative is not centered on a homosexual story or character, the visual style of heritage cinema often proves particularly 'friendly' to gay male (or women) spectators … the mise-en-scène in heritage films also places women and gay men in a privileged spectator's seat as main target audiences." Echoing Monk in her 1995 piece, Patriche uses *A Room with a View*'s male nude bathing scene as exemplary of this radical erotic and queer potentiality of heritage cinema. The film's overarching heterosexual romance cannot extinguish the "show-stopping moment" when "three naked men playfully take a dip in the 'secret lake' near the Honeychurch country estate." Although this tableau occurs within a male homosocial rather than homosexual context, "this scene sprang from the pen of the homosexual writer E.M. Forster, and its occurrence in the movie appeals primarily to gay-male spectators" (Patriche 2006, 226–7).

The estimable film critic Farran Smith Nehme addresses the enduring conventional views of Merchant Ivory. In a *Film Comment* appreciation of *A Room with a View*, she writes that it continues to be understood "as shorthand for genteel people in pretty settings," despite the fact that *Room* includes "skinny-

Figure 5
The difficulties of desire in *A Room with a View*.

dipping with frontal, flapping male nudity that's still not exactly common in mainstream cinema." And as she rightly observes, that the movie "is also lovely to look at detracts neither from its comic wisdom nor its status as one of the best movies of the 80s" (Nehme 2016).

Nehme's evocation of this moment is too good not to be shared:

The most celebrated scene is the swimming party, where George and Rev. Beebe join Lucy's brother Freddy (Rupert Graves) for a bout of joyous skinny-dipping: "Come and have a bathe," says Freddy, minutes after meeting George. "Oh, all right," is the response. First Freddy, then George, and finally the Reverend shed all those layers of clothes, and after some small mishaps ("Ugh, I've swallowed a frog" moans Freddy) they are cavorting like toddlers. It's at the moment the men jump out of the pond for a spontaneous game of stark-naked tag that they are interrupted by Lucy, her mother (Rosemary Leach), and Charlotte, who are out for a walk with (of course) Cecil. "Why not have a comfortable bath at home?" Mrs Honeychurch asks her son, after he's managed to conceal the key parts of his anatomy behind a bush.

With a sigh of relief, one concurs with Nehme's conclusions: "All these years later, surely it's time to sweep aside the preconceptions and see the film for what it is: fresh, sophisticated, and above all, passionate" (Nehme 2016). Merchant Ivory's cinema is passionate, queer, and resistant.

I want to ground my analysis of *Maurice* within the team's larger concerns with gay and lesbian representation in their adaptations of literary sources. Chief among these sources are Henry James and E.M. Forster. As a scholar who publishes in the fields of nineteenth-century American literature and film studies, with a focus on issues of gender, sexuality, and desire, I am especially drawn to Merchant Ivory films. It is well-established that Forster was a gay man, and a considerable body of criticism has focused on James as a homosexual/queer writer, beginning with Eve Kosofsky Sedgwick's still-electrifying chapter "The Beast in the Closet" on James's 1903 novella "The Beast in the Jungle." I argue that Merchant Ivory's uses of these authors' works establishes their films as significant acts of defiant gay/lesbian/queer representation.

I will turn more expansively to Forster in the next chapter, given his centrality to the present study. For now, I focus on Merchant Ivory's film *The Bostonians*, adapted from James's 1886 novel, as a key film in the team's establishment of same-sex themes as a primary area of expertise and characteristic of their special style.

Figure 6
The famous male bathing scene in *A Room with a View*.

Watershed Moment: *The Bostonians* (1984)

To consider the significance of Merchant Ivory's exploration and depiction of same-sex desire in film adaptation and historical periods, it is important to reflect on their choice of source materials. Like Forster, Henry James is recognized as a queer historical author. In reference to James's novel *Roderick Hudson* (1875), as relevant to the question of same-sex desire and gendered identity as *The Bostonians*, the critic Axel Nissen writes: "What are we to say, then, of a novel in which the characters that personify true womanhood and manhood are not irresistibly drawn to each other, choosing rather to attach themselves to the dissipated and the sensual? Where the women turn out to be manly and the men womanly? Where daughters do not necessarily love their mothers and men do not necessarily love the traits in other men that are most manly? Where four characters battle for the role of the heroine of the tale and only two of them are biologically female? Where none of the protagonists are finally united in anything remotely resembling Duffey's ideal of marriage?"[6] (Nissen 2009, 100–1). These questions index the concerns that have impelled James scholars in recent years. "Whether we approach James from the standpoint of a writer deeply conflicted regarding his own sexual identity or as a writer who increasingly came to terms with his homosexuality … we can no longer ignore how frequently the themes and images of homosexuality inform his writings," writes John Carlos Rowe (1998, 193).

Rowe argues that before Sedgwick presented her essay "The Beast in the College" at the 1984 English Institute conference,[7] "discussions of gender and sexual preferences in James's writings focused primarily on his attitudes toward nineteenth-century women's rights and his characterizations of women in his fiction." Sedgwick's pioneering work in the 1980s, which was central to the development of queer theory, "encourages us to consider the history of attitudes toward homosexuality and homosociality in the assessment of James's literary representations of gender" (Rowe 1998, 101).

Merchant Ivory's *The Bostonians*, like Sedgwick's essay, made 1984 a watershed year for queer theory and what it can illuminate in texts like James's 1886 novel. While I do not have the space to do the novel or the film anything like justice, I want to highlight some aspects of the movie that will support our discussion of *Maurice*. Jhabvala's screen adaptation hews closely to the plot of the novel. Olive Chancellor (Vanessa Redgrave), a well-born, well-off Bostonian, believes passionately in women's rights. She listens to the lecture given on the rights of women by the young Verena Tarrant (Madeleine Potter), an oratorical wunderkind. How much personal conviction Verena brings to her first-wave-feminist lectures is not clear – her huckster-mesmerist father and handler (Wesley Addy) presides over her public appearances, laying hands on her to "start her up" before she performs, as her querulous mother flutters in the background. Nevertheless, Verena speaks beautifully and stirringly, and Olive is entranced. Olive reaches out to Verena – as if for dear life – asking

Figure 7
"Will you be my friend, my friend of friends?" *The Bostonians*.
www.merchantivory.com/film/thebostonians.

her, "Will you be my friend, my friend of friends, beyond everyone, everything, forever and forever?" Jhabvala lifts this dialogue directly from the novel.

Olive and Verena seem headed for a happy Boston marriage, as close relationships between cohabiting women were called in the nineteenth century, but there's a snake in the orchard. Basil Ransom (Christopher Reeve) has come to Boston at his cousin Olive's request (she thinks he and her sister, a vain, forward society woman, might hit it off). He is a Southerner and a veteran of the Civil War – and someone whose views on social equality run fully counter to Olive's. She clearly despises him. The film begins *in medias res*, with these two staunchly opposed and formidable figures arguing "the woman question" in a carriage that is conveying them to the site of Verena's lecture.

Figure 8
The adversaries. *The Bostonians*. Internet image.
www.merchantivory.com/film/thebostonians.

Aghast at Basil's reactionary views, Olive decides he is her foe. And such he proves himself to be when both vie for possession of Verena. Despite Olive's best efforts to keep him away, and despite his belief that women at best play a "useless" role in the public sphere ("But in private? A whole lot of fun."), Basil woos Verena. Torn between Olive's and Basil's desires and efforts to possess her, Verena suffers and struggles. Finally, in the climactic sequence, when she verges on giving a speech at the Music Hall teeming with paying customers, Verena spies Basil among the spectators, panics, and declares that she cannot deliver the lecture. Olive attempts to calm the agitated Verena but cannot keep her and Basil apart. He whisks Verena away to be married, stranding Verena's entourage with the irate Music Hall lecture attendees.

Olive's intellect and her passionate commitment to the cause have contrasted sharply with her inability to speak publicly. In James's novel, Olive verges on finally speaking once Verena has gone off with Basil, though Olive expresses terror that she will be "hissed and hooted and insulted!" We never hear what she does say to the crowd; the small hope that she can and does deliver a speech is limited to the impression on Basil's part that "Olive's rush to the front" has been met by a "respectful" hush, and it was "not apparent that they were likely to hurl the benches at her." Basil is sardonically relieved to discover that "a Boston audience is not ungenerous."[8]

In the film's striking deviation from the novel, Olive does deliver a speech on the feminist cause to the remaining spectators. While we do not hear the speech in its entirety, the first several lines that we *do* hear indicate that she has found her voice at last and that the feminist cause will live on. John Carlos Rowe argues that "no feminine character" in James's fiction of the 1880s "succeeds in approaching the complexity, cultivation, and self-reliance of his own narrative voice"; "James subordinated the feminine" (Rowe 1998, 105). While I disagree with Rowe, I want to emphasize that Jhabvala and Ivory make a feminist intervention by not only giving Olive the chance to speak, a hard-won new ability, but also by creating a speech so clearly indicative of feminist progress and futures.

I mentioned in the preface that *Maurice* was a profoundly shaping film for me as a closeted college first-year. My longing to see Merchant Ivory films began with *The Bostonians*, when I was a freshman in an all-boys Catholic school, an experience that was like *Another Country* (1984) without the sex. Lured by the poster and the reviews, I asked my young, downtown-NYC-frequenting aunt Nancy to take me to see *The Bostonians*. The idea that same-sex desire was being portrayed onscreen must have osmotically conveyed itself to me, a tantalizing idea enmeshed with the allure of the period film. Other period films and television shows saturated my avid television-viewing and moviegoing life (always my refuge from the heterosexualizing constrictions of conventional society), but for some reason I *had* to see *The Bostonians*. Perhaps my determination to do so confirms that Ivory was right to cast Christopher Reeve, famous at the time for playing Superman in several movies. (Others fought against the casting, though Ivory prevailed.) But my avid moviegoing desire was largely fuelled by a longing to see Vanessa Redgrave's performance.

Watching the film again, I am struck by its emotional openness and effort to make the past seem a real, weathered, lived-in place. Complaints about Ivory's work include slow pacing, and a devout attention to objects and customs. But these very elements ground the viewer in the reality onscreen. There is nothing fetishistic about Ivory's detailed observations of history and materiality; indeed, one might say of *The Bostonians* that its presentation of nineteenth-century Boston is unglamorous and even drab. But these qualities create an atmosphere where we feel incorporated, enmeshed rather than wide-eyed. This atmosphere indicates a commitment to being in the world of the film along with the characters. Never encouraged to gush at the realm we find ourselves in, we roam it as inhabitants.

Vanessa Redgrave was not the first casting choice, as Ivory mentioned in a talkback at the Quad Cinema to celebrate the Cohen Media Group's 4K restoration and rerelease of the film in 2018; Glenn Close had been hired to play Olive.[9] It is difficult to imagine anyone other than Redgrave in the role. She was most deservedly nominated for an Oscar (as she would also be for *Howards End*).

As Ivory notes in another featurette on the Cohen Blu-ray ("The Making of *The Bostonians*"), this film was not their first gay love story (he gives that distinction to the 1975 *Autobiography of a Princess*, which includes a story about a man who falls in love with his maharajah). Nevertheless, I argue that *The Bostonians* inaugurates Merchant Ivory's period of gay and lesbian transatlantic historical cinema that extends to *Remains of the Day*. These films depict earlier historical eras charged with a heightened awareness of gender roles, sexuality, and the possibility of gay and lesbian desire.[10]

The film elaborates James's critique of compulsory heterosexuality, consistently chipping away at the natural appeal Reeve brings to Basil and depicting Verena ambivalently, as both a pawn and a willing upholder of the heterosexual social order. In contrast, Olive, no matter how alarming her wish to possess Verena may seem at times, moves closer to her rightful place as feminist heroine.

Redgrave holds nothing back in her portrayal of Olive, yearning so quickly for Verena. Her performance nakedly conveys longing, and a need to touch, caress, stroke, inhale, imbibe her younger friend. Given that the source material arguably portrays Olive and her desire as frightening, Ivory's film and

Figure 8
Merchant Ivory does Sedgwickian queer theory: between men in *A Room with a View*. https://www.adoredvintage.com/blogs/shop-journal/pretty-films-a-room-with-a-view.

Figure 10
The Bostonians critiques compulsory heterosexuality.
www.merchantivory.com/film/thebostonians.

Redgrave's interpretation humanize the character and facilitate our connection with her. In a scene late in the film, Olive races madly about after nightfall
in search of Verena, convinced that she has drowned during an illicit boating
adventure with Basil. Finally, she discovers a dishevelled and muted Verena
waiting for her in the seaside house where they're summering. Speaking no
words, Olive approaches her and essentially collapses into her, kissing and ca-
ressing her. They kiss; their tresses and bodies merge. It's erotic and sensual
and desperate. In terms of same-sex desire, Ivory says in the "Making Of" featurette, "we went as far as we could go." The sheer, overwhelming longing for
physical as well as emotional connection between same-gender lovers emerges
as a profoundly affecting theme that unites *The Bostonians* and *Maurice*.

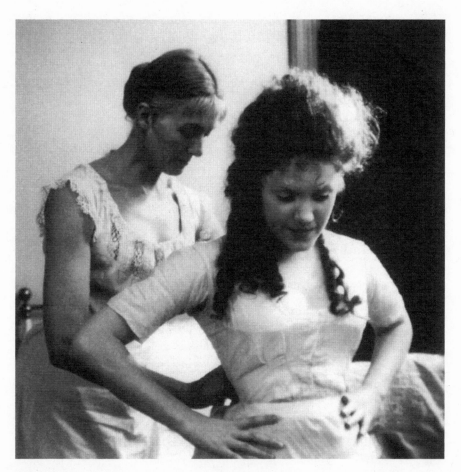

Figure 11
Ivory explains of lesbian themes in *The Bostonians*: "We went as far as we could go." www.merchantivory.com/film/thebostonians.

Queering and Fearing the 1980s: *Brideshead, Another Country, My Beautiful Laundrette*, Margaret Thatcher, and AIDS

During the grim years of the 1980s, when Ronald Reagan and Margaret Thatcher were in power and AIDS ravaged society, gays and lesbians and gender-nonconforming people were targeted by these leaders for special persecution – Reagan through a colossal wall of silence that dwarfed and silenced the realities of the AIDS epidemic, Thatcher by vocally attacking the gay community. Thatcher gave an infamous speech in 1987 explicitly attacking gays, and her Conservative government made Section 28 (also called Clause 28) law in 1988. Section 28 made the perceived promotion of homosexuality illegal, meaning for example that it was forbidden to discuss gay topics in classrooms. The law was finally repealed in England, Scotland, and Wales between 2000 and 2003.

David M. Rayside notes that the Section 28 amendment was passed by the Conservative majorities in the House of Commons and the Lords "despite considerable protest in London and other major cities, and despite widespread condemnation of the legislation as repressive in general and anti-gay in particular." Indeed, in 1990, "the Conservative government introduced a Criminal Justice Bill that included a section which classed as 'serious sex crimes' various forms of private consensual gay sex, and increased the prohibitions on such same-sex displays of affection as kissing in public" (Rayside 1992, 121).

In the United States, the Supreme Court made a momentous decision in the 1986 *Bowers v. Hardwick*: acts of sodomy were not protected by the Constitution and any states could outlaw those practices. The decision would be overturned in 2003 in the landmark *Lawrence v. Texas* case, a precursor to the court's legalization of same-sex marriage in 2015.

Government inaction and homophobic rebuke added immensely to the already unimaginable, well-nigh indescribable suffering, loss, and terror of the first AIDS decade. One has only to watch the searing and dynamic French film *BPM* (Robin Campillo, 2017), which explores the impact of AIDS and the activist efforts of ACT UP in France; Ryan Murphy's film version of Larry Kramer's 1985 play *The Normal Heart* (2014); and documentaries such as *We Were Here* (David Weissman, 2011), which chronicles the HIV/AIDS crisis in San Francisco, to be reminded – if reminder is needed – of the harrowing difficulties of this period before antiviral drugs effective at slowing down the progression of HIV were introduced in the latter half of the 1990s.

Despite the horrors of Thatcher and Reagan and AIDS, the 1980s were notable for a startling proliferation of gay-themed films, television series, and media. Some of it was fairly lowbrow (the campy ABC nighttime soap *Dynasty*, which aired almost throughout the decade, from 1981 to 1989), but a great deal of it was exciting – evidence of an inspired gay artistry thriving in the face of possible annihilation.

Subversive gay filmmakers of the 1980s like Derek Jarman, Marlon Riggs, Pedro Almodóvar, Patricia Rozema, and Monica Treut paved the way for Todd Haynes, Isaac Julien, Gregg Araki, Tom Kalin, Rose Troche, Gus Van Sant, Cheryl Dunye, and others who comprised the New Queer Cinema of the 1990s. Almodóvar's by turns sexy, harrowing, and heartbreaking *Law of Desire* (1987), the worthy subject of a wonderful Queer Film Classics volume (2009) by José Quiroga, bears special mention for its affecting and adrenalized depiction of the pains of unrequited love and the exhilaration of finally experiencing romantic and sexual fulfillment with the beloved; along these lines, *Law of Desire* and *Maurice* are sibling texts, born the same year.

In the featurettes on the 2017 Cohen Media Group Blu-ray of *Maurice*, James Ivory extensively discusses the difficulties he had in getting *Maurice* financed and distributed. Surprisingly, though, he at times also reported that he did *not* encounter difficulties. One reason for a lack of difficulty would be the worldwide success of *A Room with a View*, and another would be the devastation of the AIDS crisis. Given the obvious devastation on the gay community wrought by AIDS, no one would have openly condemned the movie – "no one would have dared," in Ivory's words. As I discuss in the last chapter, *Maurice* certainly encountered a mixed critical reaction at the time of its release from both mainstream and gay-activist critics. Still, as Ivory notes, it was clear that many people loved the resonant and revelatory film immediately.

Maurice, in other words, did not exist in a vacuum, not within Merchant Ivory's oeuvre nor within the decade's cinematic offerings. Three contemporaneous British works particularly complement *Maurice*. Establishing period drama as rife with gay possibilities, the landmark 1981 television series *Brideshead Revisited*, an adaptation of Evelyn Waugh's 1945 novel, primarily directed by directed by Charles Sturridge (with Michael Lindsay-Hogg), was a transatlantic phenomenon, the height of public television production. In part, this series about a great aristocratic family is a gay love story. Charles Ryder (Jeremy Irons) and Lord Sebastian Flyte (Anthony Andrews) meet and fall in love at Oxford in 1922; one can read much into the narrative as presented although no explicit sex scenes exist between the men. The contrast between two deeply handsome and appealing young men, the yin and yang dark-haired look of Charles and blond one of Sebastian, prefigures the contrast between blond Maurice Hall (James Wilby) and dark-haired Clive Durham (Hugh Grant) and Alec Scudder (Rupert Graves) in *Maurice*. (It was Ivory's decision to make Maurice, dark-haired in the novel, blond.) Similarly, Charles's middle-class background in contrast to Sebastian's aristocratic one dovetails with the relationship between middle-class Maurice and high-born Clive, and between Maurice and working-class Alec.

The British romantic historical drama *Another Country* (1984) also paved the way for *Maurice*. Adapted by Julian Mitchell from his play of the same name and directed by Marek Kanievska, a queer-content-friendly director who would later direct the 1987 film version of Brett Easton Ellis's bisexually oriented novel *Less Than Zero* (1985), the film stars Rupert Everett (in what remains his most indelible screen role), Colin Firth (his screen debut), and Cary Elwes. The story is based on the real-life Cambridge Spies (Donald Maclean, Guy Burgess, Harold Philby, and Anthony Blunt) who passed state secrets to the Soviet Union beginning in the 1930s. Everett's Guy Bennett (a name clearly recalling Guy Burgess) is the protagonist within a dynamic en-

Figure 12
Rupert Everett and Colin Firth in *Another Country*. Twitter, @criterionchannl.

semble. The movie has a framing device of an interview with the aged Bennett, who now lives in Moscow. As he explains why he betrayed England to a female reporter, we shift to the past, a public school, reminiscent of Eton and Winchester, in the 1930s. Lordly, droll, tall, and imposing, Guy chafes perpetually against the petty tyrannies of his peers in power. In an atmosphere that recalls *The Lord of the Flies*, the school is run only peripherally by adults. The students, house captains, and the two top prefects, or "Gods," wield all the power, controlling their underlings in militaristic fashion. Early on, an adult supervisor catches and reports on two young male students, one from a different house, masturbating together. One of the boys dies by suicide, setting the plot (about who will become a God) in motion.

The film offers an incisive, haunting exploration of the British school system and its simultaneous promotion and rigid policing of homosexual desire.

Homosexuality, the film makes evident, is an implicit aspect of English pub-lic-school life, but one that must be kept completely subterranean, with the understanding that boys will eventually grow out of their same-sex attractions and become properly heterosexual and upstanding citizens.

Guy chafes against the constrictive system that binds the students to their authoritarian doubles, but he wants to be a God himself. The student leaders tolerate his acid wit and louche demeanour because he blackmails them, threatening to reveal their mutual sexual trysts. Guy's best friend, Tommy Judd (Firth), isn't gay, but he is a Marxist who detests the system even more than Guy. Guy submits to the authority of the masters and prefects only to protect the identity of his young lover, James Harcourt (Elwes). When the house captain Fowler (Tristan Oliver) intercepts a love letter from Guy to James, Guy submits to a caning rather than reveal James's identity and en-danger him. (The caning is a brutal and, truth be told, kinky scene.)

The boys, oppressed as they are, want to maintain the status quo, including the availability of same-sex sexual relations provided they remain clandestine. As one student puts it, if only the man who discovered the boys having a mas-turbatory tryst and reported them had been "an old boy" – in other words someone who'd gone through the system, possibly indulged in homo-activity, but knew to keep it quiet – the scandalous suicide of the outed boy would never have occurred.

Given the year of its release, *Another Country* is remarkable for its depiction of same-sex love.[11] Guy refuses to hide his homosexuality, declaring to Tommy that he will never love women. Guy's posh background does give him some freedoms. In one scene, he invites James to an elaborate dinner out. James worries that their cover will be blown when the adult authorities spot them there, but Guy assures him that the school's employees could never afford to dine in such a restaurant; his means keep them safe. We essentially watch the two beautiful young men falling in love over dinner. In another scene, set late at night, dark-haired Guy and blond James sit in a canoe, away from everyone else, their arms tightly clasped around one another. Another country, indeed, in 1984.

My Beautiful Laundrette (1985) was directed by English director and producer Stephen Frears from a screenplay by Hanif Kureishi, a Pakistani and English playwright, screenwriter, filmmaker, and novelist who is bisexual. One of the great films of the decade, *Laundrette*, like *Another Country*, laid the groundwork for *Maurice*. As a team, Frears and Kureishi double Ivory and Merchant. Like *A Room with a View* in the same year, *Laundrette* features a breakout performance by Daniel Day-Lewis. In *Room*, he plays the desiccated and prissy pseudo-intellectual Cecil Vyse, set to marry the heroine Lucy Honeychurch (Helena Bonham Carter). Day-Lewis took the opportunity to demonstrate his range and ran with it by giving a performance in *Laundrette* quite distinct from the one he gives in *Room*. His petty hoodlum Johnny has a punker look, spiky hair dyed blond on top, with dark roots beneath.

Johnny is the childhood friend of the film's protagonist, Omar Ali (Gordon Warnecke), a young Anglo-Pakistani man-on-the-make who looks after his father, Hussein, an alcoholic who was once a prominent journalist in Bombay. (He is played by the great Roshan Seth, with a look in his eyes of both drollery and infinite sadness.) In a chance reunion, Omar encounters Johnny again after many years. A gang begins shouting anti-immigrant profanities at Omar and his family members in their car one night; Johnny appears to be leading this gang. Yet despite the mayhem, Omar and Johnny reconnect, and there is a palpable buzz in their interaction. Frears uses a stylized, expressionistic aesthetic to convey the magical quality of Omar and Johnny's chance reunion.

Eventually, the enterprising Johnny goes to work for his wheeling-and-dealing, energetic paternal uncle Nasser. Nasser is played by the marvellously likable Saeed Jaffrey, no stranger to Merchant Ivory films. Fairly quickly, Omar is successfully managing a laundrette and has hired Johnny as his bodyguard of sorts and as an employee of the laundrette. Eventually, Johnny must fight off former gang members, who beat him up badly.

None of these tricky complications stop Johnny and Omar from becoming lovers (perhaps resuming a romantic and sexual relationship). In the most famous shot in the film, Johnny surreptitiously licks Omar behind the ear in the daylight just out of eyeshot of the rowdy gang members. The fusion of gay desire and racial politics, the melancholia of the immigrant experience and the brazen racism of English society, all make *Laundrette* ahead of its time and an enduringly fresh, vibrant work.

As Gary Goldstein correctly summarizes in an interview with Ivory and James Wilby to mark the occasion of the Cohen Media Group restoration and theatrical rerelease of *Maurice* in 2017, "It's not as if the 1980s hadn't already produced a string of features involving meaningful gay male characters: *Making Love*, *Kiss of the Spider Woman*, *My Beautiful Laundrette* and others. But the lush, dignified *Maurice*, with its share of man-on-man smooches, full-frontal male nudity, gay lovemaking and unabashed declarations of same-sex desire, as well as a main character who was ultimately affirmative and unwavering about his homosexuality (during a time when it was a criminal offense, no less), landed a unique place in then-contemporary gay culture" (Goldstein 2017).

Merchant Ivory's cinema thematizes the closet and its experiential and outward effects. As does E.M. Forster's novel *Maurice*, to which we now turn.

Chapter 2

Portrait of a Gay Man as a Surprise to Himself: Forster's *Maurice*

This is a propitious time for studying E.M. Forster's signal role as a gay artist whose work continues to spark the queer imagination. In 2021, Matthew López became the first Latino playwright to win the Tony Award for best play. In *The Inheritance*, López reworks Forster's great novel *Howards End* to offer a sweeping account of the AIDS crisis that meditates on the intergenerational ties between gay men. Damon Galgut's 2014 *Arctic Summer*, which takes its title from the novel that Forster began writing and left unfinished in order to write *Maurice*, makes Forster himself the protagonist and charts his sexual self-realization. Wendy Moffat's superlative *A Great Unrecorded History: A New Life of E.M. Forster* (2010) reframes the author as a homosexual visionary, breaking new ground and illuminating the significance of his longstanding queer themes. William di Canzio's lyrical, erotic, haunting novel *Alec* (2021) is a sequel to *Maurice*, picking up where Forster left off and exploring the lovers' confrontation with the Great War, in which both serve. Forster here, too, becomes a character, the "Morgan" who teaches the protagonist about the arts.

Forster's *Maurice* was treated derisively when it was published in 1971, for example in Cynthia Ozick's notoriously homophobic pan in *Commentary*, where she treats the novel as sickly special pleading. The novel has repeatedly encountered patronizing and hostile criticism as a lesser work, "sub-Forster," as Jhabvala said to Merchant and Ivory when explaining why she did not want to adapt the novel. Reviewing the Ivory film in the *Sunday Times* (London), George Perry sniffed, "*Maurice* is essentially a cold, shallow, dated exercise. Just like the book, in fact." David Ansen's contemporaneous review of the film strikes an equally characteristic note: "The Merchant/Ivory *Maurice* is a lovely, languorous and problematic movie. If it isn't on the same inspired level as their adaptation of Forster's *A Room with a View*, the reason may be simple: their source isn't as good. As filmmakers, they've always prided themselves on their literary fidelity, and in making *Maurice*, a little more creative infidelity might have been profitable" (Ansen 1987, 76).

"Most Forster fans have not read the original novel, largely because of the hostile discourse that appeared as soon as it was published," writes Alexander Chee in his review of *Alec*. "The novelist Edmund White recalls reading *Maurice* only after seeing the film, since he had interviewed two of the actors around the time the film came out. He had been put off by the critical condemnation of the novel. I confess I did much the same" (Chee 2021).

Though rather obtuse in his hostility to Merchant Ivory, David Leavitt does offer one of the best treatments of the novel in his introduction to the Penguin Classics edition. On Ozick's callous response, he writes, "What she seems to miss is *Maurice*'s sex appeal. Over and over Forster hymns his solidity, his bulk, his athleticism, noting with a distinct tone of longing that he 'would have been a good lover. He could have given and taken serious pleasure.' In that potentiality lies the key to Maurice's allure" (Leavitt 2005, xv).

Given that I consider *Maurice* a great novel, and because of its significance as Forster's chief contribution to queer liberation, I offer a close reading of it in this chapter, joining contemporary critics such as the contributors to the volume *Twenty-First-Century Readings of E.M. Forster's Maurice* and novelists William di Canzio and David Leavitt in embracing Forster's underappreciated masterpiece. In so doing, I lay the groundwork for appreciating James Ivory's.

Figure 13
Photograph of E.M. Forster in
1947. Archives of American Art,
Smithsonian Institution, Flickr.

Forster and *Maurice*

In proleptic defiance of the sturdy twentieth-century tradition of dire fates
for gay protagonists, E.M. Forster decided to give his heroes Maurice Hall
(Hill in many early drafts) and Alec Scudder a happy ending. As he writes in
in his 1960 "Terminal Note" that accompanied the 1971 publication of *Maurice*,
"A happy ending was imperative. I shouldn't have bothered to write otherwise.
I was determined that in fiction anyway two men should fall in love and remain in it for the ever and ever that fiction allows, and in this sense Maurice
and Alec still roam the greenwood" (Forster 2006,[1] 250).[2]

If one imagines the novel written in the first person, Maurice might offer his version of *Jane Eyre*'s famous line "Reader, I married him": "Reader, I share with him always," to use Alec's, and Forster's, euphemism for sexual love. The happy ending he gives Maurice and Alec reveals Forster's vision of a definitive one: a fulfilling, mutually loving, and sexually satisfying relationship between men. Forster finds meaning in the marriage plot, evoking Jane Austen and her belief in hard-won marital union as the proper reward for likable, basically good people who've struggled toward and suffered for this joyous tie.

The happy ending is itself a controversial subject, as we will discuss. Among *Maurice*'s early readers, Lytton Strachey found the relationship between middle-class Maurice and his first love, the well-born Clive Durham, "extraordinarily well-done," but found the mixed-class Maurice-Alec romance unconvincing, and complained of its "Sherwood Forest ending" (Gardner 1999, xxvi).

Forster's insistence on giving Maurice and Alec a romantic future derived from his exposure to the stirring example of a real-life gay relationship. The upper-middle-class and Cambridge-educated poet and social activist Edward Carpenter was a homosexual visionary and polymath who shared a life with his lover George Merrill, a working-class man twenty-two years his junior. Forster's class-defying love story between middle-class Maurice and working-class Alec emerged from his encounter with the pair. As Forster explains in his "Terminal Note": "In its original form, which it still almost retains, *Maurice* dates from 1913. It was a direct result of a visit to Edward Carpenter at Milthorpe. Carpenter had a prestige that cannot be understood today … He was a socialist who ignored industrialism and a simple-lifer with an independent income and a Whitmannic poet … and a believer in the Love of Comrades, whom he sometimes called Uranians. It was this last aspect of him that attracted me in my loneliness." Forster reports that his "second or third visit" to Millthorpe made a "profound impression" and touched "a creative spring." George Merrill "also touched my backside – gently and just above the buttocks. I believe he touched most people's." The memorable experience was "as much psychological as physical. It seemed to go straight through the small of my back into my ideas." That touch on the backside led him immediately to begin writing *Maurice* when he visited his mother at Harrowgate, where she was "taking a cure" (249–50). A desire to avoid his mother's disapproval was a contributing factor to Forster's steadfast refusal to publish the book in his lifetime.

That Maurice and Alec embark on a relationship at the narrative's end has been viewed as an embarrassing wish-fulfillment fantasy indicative of the novel's wrongheaded, naïve qualities. Given this critical opprobrium, Claire Monk, who has written at length on the novel as well as the heritage film tradition that Merchant Ivory typifies, makes a notable intervention: "*Maurice*'s (sly, queer, arguably deceptive) textual appearance of narrative and generic 'simplicity' – its directness, its generic accessibility, Forster's utopian insistence on a happy ending – stands as its great strength." These qualities account for "*Maurice*'s survival, its extraordinary continuing circulation and popularity in twenty-first century media culture, its availability to young-adult readerships and its continuing relevance and political, affective and aesthetic power" (Monk 2020, 230–1).

By the time Forster wrote *Maurice*, most of his famous novels had already been published: *Where Angels Fear to Tread* (1905), *The Longest Journey* (1907), *A Room with a View* (1908); the great *Howards End* (1910). *A Passage to India* (1924) lay ahead. Like *Howards End*, with its famous dictum "only connect," *Maurice* "is about the stranglehold of social class," which prevents relations between those of different classes and keeps eros safely safeguarded against difference. Forster created "a revolutionary new genre" in *Maurice* that made good on the author's belief that "a happy ending was imperative."

Forster's long-time friend, the writer Christopher Isherwood – author of *A Single Man* and *The Berlin Stories*, the basis for the musical *Cabaret* – had long exhorted Forster to publish *Maurice*. By 1952, Forster agreed that Isherwood should be entrusted with shepherding *Maurice*'s publication, albeit after its author's death. Consulting with his friend the English publisher John Lehmann – associated with the Bloomsbury Group of Virginia and Leonard

Woolf and the Hogarth Press – Isherwood brought *Maurice* to published life after its several decades as a private text passed hand to hand in Forster's inner circle.[3] Preparing for the posthumous publication of Forster's masterwork of gay freedom, Isherwood turned to Lehmann while scanning the droves of critical work focused on Forster and opined, "Of course all those books have got to be re-written. Unless you start with the fact that he was homosexual, nothing's any good at all" (Moffat 2010, 20).

Forster's view that homophobia kept a constrictive lock on sexual expression can hardly be disputed given the rise in postwar arrests of gay men in the UK. The harrowing case of the English mathematician Alan Turing, a Second World War hero famous for Nazi codebreaking as well as the development of artificial intelligence, provides an exemplum. He devised, in a 1951 paper, a legendary test called "The Imitation Game" to determine whether a computer could pass for a human. Despite his innovative as well as patriotic accomplishments, Turing was persecuted for being a gay man and forced to undergo chemical castration. He died by suicide in 1954.

Some progress was being made, as signalled by the 1957 Wolfenden report's recommendations that homosexual activities between consenting adults should no longer be prosecuted. With some bitterness, Forster predicted in the "Terminal Note" that the Wolfenden report's recommendations would be "indefinitely rejected," police prosecutions allowed to persist, and, referring to Maurice's would-be-lover-turned-straight Clive Durham, "Clive on the bench will continue to sentence Alec in the dock. Maurice may get off" (Forster 2006, 255). The eighty-eight-year-old Forster witnessed the passing of the Sexual Offenses Act in 1967, which legalized sex "between men who desired each other, were alone in a house, and over twenty-one" (although only if they lived in England and Wales) (Moffat 2010, 19).

Forster's novel must be understood in terms of its "complex history" in the years "between 1913 and 1971: the product of fifty-seven years of private circulation, and intermittent but protracted textual revisions, during which divergent drafts were read by multiple 'peer reviewers'" (Monk 2020, 231). The mazy history of the novel's various versions is expertly and expansively documented by Philip Gardner in his masterly "Editor's Introduction" to the Abinger edition of *Maurice* (London: André Deutsch, 1999). He writes, "Any edition of *Maurice* must obviously take into account Forster's second, and third, thoughts about a novel which mattered deeply to him." The 1971 edition first published by Edward Arnold and edited by P.N. Furbank aimed to honour these intentions. *Maurice*, however, existed in various states of revision, the most significant years of these alterations occurring in 1914, 1932, and 1959 (Gardner 1999, l). Given that the 1971 edition was the one that James Ivory and Ismail Merchant and their team adapted when they made the film, it will be the text I use throughout this book.

Maurice Hall is in many ways an unlikely subject for heroism, perhaps especially gay heroism. Even more so than in Merchant Ivory's adaptation, Forster's Maurice is blinkered, classist, reactionary, and quite comfortable with his privilege. He treats his sisters abominably and at times seems almost "soulless." Clive Durham marries Anne Woods and takes up politics. When Maurice visits Clive for the first time since his wedding and finally meets Anne, she mentions that the new rector Mr Borenius agitates on behalf of the poor, and often comes by to "scold Clive about the housing" (167). Maurice's response to these matters is telling. "'I've had to do with the poor too,' said Maurice, taking a piece of cake, 'but I can't worry over them. One must give them a leg up for the sake of the country generally, that's all. They haven't our feelings. They don't suffer as we should in their place … The poor don't want pity. They only really like me when I've got gloves on and am knocking about'" (167–8). Anne looks at him with some disapproval and even chastises him for being "horrible," but secretly thinks that she has found the right stockbroker in Maurice. Forster makes it clear that Maurice's "biting recklessness" in this moment stems from his irritation that Clive had not planned to be there when Maurice arrives.

One of Forster's strategies, both plangent and subversive, is to make Maurice's homosexuality and self-acceptance and his love for Alec, which synthesizes both, what save him. Falling in love with Clive Durham's gamekeeper Alec Scudder, Maurice defies class as well as gender boundaries. Clive's horrified response to Maurice's declaration that he loves Alec encapsulates the social opprobrium Maurice now willingly risks. The same Maurice who had discussed the poor as if a different species from the upper-class English now champions, with a sense of wonder, Alec as someone who "sacrificed his career for my sake ... without a guarantee," someone that Maurice "will give up anything for" (244).

The novel focuses its first attention on the adolescent Maurice Hall at preparatory school and opens with a scene that elliptically conveys a sense of Maurice's queer apartness. Mr Ducie, a senior schoolmaster, has an eye on Hall, one of the older boys who part from the school when they are fourteen, headed for public school (Maurice is older than fourteen). Hall wants to "take his last walk with his school-fellows," but Mr Ducie wants to walk with him privately and have "the 'good talk,'" introducing Maurice to the world of adult heterosexual intercourse (10). Forster does not make this explicit, but clearly Mr Ducie sees that Hall, unlike his schoolfellows, particularly needs this introduction.

Whatever Maurice reported to the other schoolmaster about wanting to walk with his classmates, when Mr Ducie announces, "I'm going to walk with Hall alone," Maurice is "triumphant" as he springs to the schoolmaster's side. The older man and the boy walk along a sandy beach while the other boys scamper "up on the cliff" (11). Mr Ducie asks Maurice, "What do you suppose the world – the world of grown-up people is like?" Maurice when further pressed explains that his family consists of his mother and his sisters Ada and Kitty, his father having recently died from pneumonia. (Though Maurice, conventionally attractive and athletic, is physically quite unlike Forster himself, the author gave him autobiographical qualities such as being fatherless and raised by a widowed mother. Forster's father Eddie died when his son was not yet two, leaving his mother Lily "a twenty-five-year-old widow" [Moffat 2010, 26].) Mr Ducie presses hard on the point that Maurice has no older brothers or uncles, concluding, "So you don't know many men?" (12).

In an interesting detail, Mr Ducie prefaces his lesson to Maurice with a made-up story that Ducie's father had shared the same lesson with him when he was a boy. Ducie's father actually "never told him anything" (13). But the schoolmaster proceeds, "very simply and kindly," to explain to Maurice "the mystery of sex": "He spoke of male and female, created by God in the begin-ning in order that the earth might be peopled, and of the period when the male and the female receive their powers." He then draws diagrams in the sand using his walking stick (13). Maurice watches Ducie etch his sandy sexual diagrams earnestly but "dully," feeling no corresponding response to the etch-ings even though they "related to his own body." His "torpid brain would not awake" (14).

After more grand pronouncements on Love and Life, and some dutiful how-to questions from Maurice, Mr Ducie praises the "ideal man – chaste with asceticism. He sketched the glory of Woman" and explained that loving and protecting her was a man's highest duty in life (14). His panegyrics to het-erosexual and gender normalcy reach a climax: "All's right with the world. Male and female! Ah, wonderful!" Tellingly, Maurice remarks, "I think I shall not marry" (15). Maurice's remark gets its own paragraph, a small island of barely permissible defiance standing apart from Ducie's ecstatic, grandiosely conventional commentary. Adding a comic note that Merchant Ivory ampli-fies, after the boy and his schoolmaster have walked some more, Ducie sud-denly realizes that "I never scratched out those infernal drawings" (15).

The chapter concludes surprisingly. Maurice realizes something suddenly: "for an instant of time, the boy despised him": "'Liar, coward, he's told me nothing'" (15). Maurice's alternately cheerful and plodding comportment never prepares us for his burst of rebellious contempt for the well-meaning – perhaps – and quietly aggressive Mr Ducie and his simultaneously com-manding and ephemeral lessons in the sand.

Forster takes a wry but strong stand against the compulsory heterosexual indoctrination that continues to undergird society even to this day when sexual and gender difference and variety are more visible and defended and, arguably, contested than ever before. Moreover, the nascent sense that he is "different from the others" (to evoke the title of Richard Oswald's famous 1919 Weimar Republic–era silent German film on the love that dare not speak its name) gives Maurice something: an intransigence that leads him, bland as he is, to resist an overarching gender and sexual system presented by the authority figure as inescapable. And who would ever dream of escaping it, clothed in idealizing glory as it is? That Maurice does imagine escape gives him character and spirit enough to resist, to say, "I shall not" in the face of "You must" and "You will."

When Mr Ducie presses Maurice about not having men in his life (which will become a problem for Maurice in ways unimaginable, or not so unimaginable, later), the fourteen-year-old talks about his mother's coachman Howell and "George," the most recent hire in the procession of young men employed by the coachman. Coming back to his mother's home, near London, Maurice soon asks her where George is, receiving (the second time he poses the question to his mother) the answer that George has left because he has aged out of the job – "Howell always changes the boy every two years" (17). A few more line items in his mother's updates to him proceed before Maurice suddenly lets out a sob, not directly connected to any cause. His mother haplessly tries to comfort him but soon joins in his tears, out of sympathy for him and because she cannot "make him happy." Pressed for an explanation for his spontaneous tears, Maurice can only repeat "I don't know" (18).

Later that night, Maurice lies in bed. Alert and apprehensive, he begins thinking about George, recalling him. "Something stirred in the unfathomable depths of his heart." He whispers George's name twice. The narrator pointedly asks, "Who was George? Nobody – just a common servant" (19–20). This memory and spiritual summons of George is a "sorrow" that Maurice accesses, which allows the troubled boy to sleep. Forster suggests that unconscious desire for the coachman's departed assistant fuels the young hero's night terrors. Yet in weeping over George (as he must be doing earlier) and now crying out for him, Maurice gains insight into his "torpid" inner life, learning who he is and how to live by gaining clarity about his desire. The film does not include Maurice's early fixation on George, using the beach sex-education scene with Ducie as prologue and cutting to Maurice at university.

Maurice will need some time to find this clarity. When, at nineteen, he talks to their neighbour Dr Barry about his future, Dr Barry easily fills Maurice's checklist out himself: Cambridge, followed by working as his father did at the Stock Exchange, a place already secured for him by his father's old partner there – and why *wouldn't* things go well for Maurice (26)? The only wrench thrown into the works is his homosexuality, which awaits its first active expression at Cambridge. Dr Barry, continuing a pattern of older males treating younger ones in a suspect manner, regards Maurice with competitive contempt. Like Mr Ducie, Dr Barry imparts lessons in compulsory heterosexuality: "Man that is born of woman must go with woman if the human race is to continue." Remembering Ducie's diagrams, Maurice experiences a "violent repulsion" and longs to be a boy once more, "half awake for ever by the colourless sea" (28).

By the time he gets to Cambridge, Maurice is thoroughly convinced that "in all creation there could be no one as vile as himself" (30). He meets a flamboyant student named Risley. Maurice regards him ambivalently but thinks he can learn from Risley, "capering on the summit" of the mountains of inexperience and fear that surround and dwarf Maurice (34). Calling on Risley one night, Maurice instead meets Clive Durham. In their early exchanges, discussing music and other intellectual matters, Maurice feels intimidated by Clive's "unmoved" demeanour. Clive "shook out the falsities, and approved the rest. What hope for Maurice who was nothing but falsities?" (39). In the face of Clive's self-confident tranquility and orderliness, Maurice feels fraudulent (38).

In behaviour we might call stalkerish today, Maurice camps out in the courtyard one night, waiting for a glimpse of Clive. Finally, back in his room,

Figure 14
Cambridge University offers an idyllic and constrictive atmosphere that kindles
Maurice and Clive's romance.

Clive hears Maurice shouting goodnight at him from below. Summoning up
all his courage, Maurice asks Clive if he fancies some tea. No, he doesn't, Clive
responds. Disaster looms … But what about some whiskey? The question
"leaps" from Maurice's mouth: "Have you a drop?" (39). Clive in his ground
floor room offers Maurice a drink, which he believes he must gulp down since
Clive only invited him out of politeness. Maurice quickly heads back to his
own room, but then goes out into the courtyard again, his nerves abuzz. He
falls asleep outside and gets rained on. But it doesn't matter: "his heart had
lit never to be quenched again, and one thing in him at last was real" (40).

It's got to be real – that would seem to be the message here. Maurice threatens to lead a Thoreauvian life of quiet desperation, muddling through university and his stockbroker's job. But he is saved by desire.

Forster depicts Maurice and Clive's growing awareness of mutual desire as inextricable from the homosocial environment of university life. Their physical proximity to one another, Clive seated at the base of Maurice's chair, even Maurice's stroking of his friend's hair, never alarms their friendship circle. The insecurity Maurice always feels with Clive leads him to insist that he thinks and feels, which he worries Clive does not know. They debate religious matters, Clive taking an atheistic view, Maurice, who perhaps finds religion a respite from Clive-obsession, defending the Trinity.

These trinitarian controversies lead us to one of the best-known moments in the text. During the dean's translation class in Greek attended by Maurice and Clive, the dean instructs, "Omit: a reference to the unspeakable vice of the Greeks." Later, Clive chides the dean for his hypocrisy, arguing that the ancient Greeks were indeed generally "that way inclined," and he asks Maurice if he has read *The Symposium*. He has not. But now Maurice knows that this unspeakable subject can be mentioned out loud. When Clive speaks of it "in the middle of the sunlit court," Maurice inhales a newfound "breath of liberty" (51).

A historical aside: As Louis Crompton discusses in his excellent book *Byron and Greek Love: Homophobia in 19th Century England*, the handsome young poetic genius Percy Bysshe Shelley fretted over the idea of homosexuality in ancient Greece (Crompton 1985, 284–311). The poet expanded on his views on Greek homosexuality and pederasty in his essay *A Discourse on the Manners of the Antient Greeks Relative to the Subject of Love*.

Shelley could not wrap his mind around the idea of sodomy, an important component of Greek education, specifically the idea that an older man (the *erastes*) would penetrate a younger (the *eromenos*). (Typically, we should note, the sex between the older man and the young man he initiated into knowledge was intercrural, between the thighs, rather than anal-penetrative.) How could such a "detestable violation" commonly occur in a civilization that was the pinnacle of human achievement? Indeed, he concluded that it could not, and that other means of same-sex sexual gratification were sought (Worthen 2019, 196).

Nevertheless, Shelley translated Plato's *Symposium*, calling it *The Banquet*, because he was disgusted by the Christian piety that expurgated sexual content such as homosexuality and pederasty from ancient texts. Alas, Mary Shelley, the poet's wife and the equally famous author of *Frankenstein*, published expurgated versions of *A Discourse* and his translation of *The Symposium* in 1840. She excised "substantial portions of Alcibiades' account of his sexual relationship with Socrates" from his translation of *The Symposium*. It was not until 1949 that Shelley's original, unexpurgated texts of *The Symposium* and *A Discourse* were published (Bieri 2005, 69–70). All these tensions in the reception of ancient Greek texts echo in *Maurice*. At the same time, the ancient world provided a foundation for the celebration of homosexual aesthetics in the late nineteenth century. Oscar Wilde and Walter Pater, among others, promulgated a queer Hellenism that provided a powerful vent for homoerotic desire.

The term's end sends Maurice home, where his mother and sisters irritate him by mispronouncing Clive's last name and failing to take Maurice's newfound atheism seriously. Maurice contradicts his mother's sense of him as "the image of his father," continuing the pattern of Oedipal opposition. Meanwhile, Maurice and Clive correspond, the latter never responding much to Maurice's carefully expressed "shades of feeling," yet writing letters equally long. Maurice fetishizes these epistles as physical talismans, keeping them in his pockets always, transferring them from one suit to the next, "even pinning them in his pyjamas" before bed (52–3).

A distressing episode follows when Maurice tries to simulate normal hetero behavior and acts very badly towards a friend of Mrs Hall and Ada, Gladys Olcott, who is visiting the family. Maurice decides to act the part of the "domineering male" and makes a pass at her. He presses Miss Olcott's hand – and it's a most unwelcome gesture.

Now, Maurice is no eyesore. He has become attractive and athletic, which cures his clumsy qualities. The problem is not his looks. Nor is it the woman's attitude toward such gestures. "It was not that Miss Olcott objected to having her hand pressed." Others had done so. "But she knew something was wrong. His touch revolted her. It was a corpse's." Poor Miss Olcott makes a hasty exit and heads for the train. Despite her discretion, the other Halls know that something unfortunate has occurred (54–5). Scenes involving Miss Olcott were filmed by James Ivory but left on the cutting room floor. They can, however, be seen in the series of deleted scenes in the Cohen Media Blu-ray. (I support the decision to cut this scene from the film, where it has little of the power, if the deleted scene is any indication, it does in the novel. Sometimes scenes are cut for a reason. But, as I will discuss in the next chapter, some scenes should never have been cut from the film.) In the meantime, Maurice gets on with things. He contacts his father's old business partner and quite effortlessly secures himself a position as a stockbroker: once he has "left Cambridge" he will work at Hill and Hall, Stock Brokers, "stepping into the niche that England had prepared for him" (55).

The ease with which Maurice shifts gears after treating Miss Olcott so badly is chilling. Forster makes it clear that the closet deadens the soul and the heart. Maurice's body undergoes a premature burial, leaving him a living corpse whose touch, despite his comely form, is revolting. The closet makes Maurice unthinkable not only as a heterosexual suitor but also sexual object for women. His treatment of Miss Olcott presages his horrible treatment of his sister Ada when he suspects romance brewing between her and Clive.

The next chapter condenses action that occurs in different scenes in the film. Back from "vac," Maurice and Clive awkwardly reencounter one another but swiftly rediscover their intimacy. Clive sits at Maurice's feet and he bends his seated friend's head "against his knee, as though it was a talisman for clear living." Maurice strokes Clive's hair, and repeating this gesture achieves something: "a new tenderness." Clive asks him, in reference to Miss Olcott, if there has been some trouble (57). Maurice responds that there has not been. "I thought you liked her," says Clive, to which Maurice answers, "I didn't – don't" (58).

Maurice emits "deeper sighs" as he looks up at the ceiling and reminds himself that man was created to suffer "pain and loneliness without help from heaven." That's bleaker than anything Milton hypothesizes in *Paradise Lost*. But help is imminent. Clive strokes Maurice's hair (indelibly depicted in the film, which shows Clive seated as he does this). Maurice and Clive now clasp one another. "They were lying breast against breast soon, head was on shoulder," but just when their cheeks are about to touch, their antic classmates besiege them, shrivelling their new tenderness. Later, Clive confirms that Maurice had "read *The Symposium* in the vac," in order further to confirm, "Then you understand – without me saying more." Maurice remains a bit dim even now. Obtusely, he responds, "How do you mean?" To which Clive responds, "I love you" (58).

Maurice could not react more adversely, especially given that he is no less in love himself. He chastises Clive, claiming that as "Englishmen" they must abjure "a subject absolutely beyond the limit … the worst crime in the calendar" (59). He instructs Clive never to discuss this again. But Clive has already made a hasty exit.

Maurice has long felt a torpor befogs his brain. Not yet consciously aware that his feelings for Clive run deep, he appears "insensitive" because his feelings take a long time to be understood. Clive for his part takes an "icy" sardonic approach, asking Maurice to keep knowledge of Clive's "criminal morbidity" to himself (60).

Maurice finds himself weeping profusely one night, and this outpouring is cathartic. It leads to self-discovery at last: "He loved men and always had loved them." No more would he "pretend to care about women when the only sex that attracted him was his own." The hard-won realizations that he loves men, wants to "mingle his being" with them, and loves Clive arise from losing Clive, who returns his love but has been rejected (62).

But the crisis has a very powerful effect on Maurice: it turns him into a man. A man who has discovered the power of speech. Now that he realizes what and whom he loves, Maurice longs to shout barbaric yawps attesting to the fact. But Clive, mortified, will have none of this. Clive takes the position that a degenerate like himself will depend no further on Maurice's extraordinary kindness, discretion, and sympathy. "You're beastly hard," Maurice responds (64).

Pained by all of this, Maurice solicits Clive's sympathies. They bicker anew and Maurice departs Clive's room, only to commence another rainy nighttime courtyard vigil while awaiting Clive's return. Finally, "savage, reckless, drenched with rain," he cannot hold back anymore. He will enter Clive's room. He grabs the mullioned window and is about to do so when a sound – someone saying "Maurice" – startles him awake. "His friend had called him." And laying his hands on the pillows, Maurice responds, "Clive!" (66). Part 1 of the novel ends with this oneiric reconciliation.

Part 2 opens with a chapter that answers the previous one. Forster shifts perspectives and gives Clive his focus. Through the technique of free indirect discourse, the narrator parses Clive's thoughts for us. Fascinatingly, Maurice emerges as a much sturdier piece of machinery when seen through Clive's eyes. "Hall," as Clive thinks of him, is "bourgeois, unfinished and stupid," every bit the blunt, unimaginative person we have met. But Hall offers Clive something else: a "teasing" quality that distinguishes him from Clive's social circle, who find him too "sedate." Clive enjoys being teased by Hall, "thrown about by a powerful and handsome boy." He also relishes the times when this stirring fellow strokes his hair (71).

While Maurice seems miserable during those debates about theology in the previous chapter, Clive has been experiencing them with a sense of discovery. Maurice is "affectionate, kindly," and something more. He brings to these debates an "impudence" that Clive likes. All the while Maurice develops "a peculiar and beautiful expression" that keeps sweetening the pot. Gradually but surely, Clive becomes convinced that Maurice loves him, which has "unloosed his own love" for Maurice (72). When Maurice rejects Clive's declaration of love, it genuinely stuns and stings him.

But by the end of the chapter, brash Maurice is climbing into Clive's room through the window at night. Pressing his weight upon sleeping Clive and waking him leads to Clive declaring his love again, to which Maurice economically responds, "I you" and kisses him. This is no longer a dream fulfilment but an actual event, one faithfully depicted in the film (74). Now on the same romantic page, Maurice and Clive take a day trip to the countryside in a motor bicycle–cum–sidecar, leaving Cambridge and disapproving Dean Cornwallis behind. The staid-seeming Maurice, reminded he has a lecture by the dean whom they careen past, rudely retorts, "I overslept" (75).

As the young men make their way to the "grassy embankment" where they picnic, a bold transformation occurs. "They became a cloud of dust, a stench, and a roar to the world" and "cared for no one," being "outside humanity," a state of otherness that, if intruded upon by death, would only continue "their pursuit of a retreating horizon" (76). Suddenly, Maurice and Clive become an outlaw queer couple like the one in Gregg Araki's New Queer Cinema indie movie classic *The Living End* (1992). Their burgeoning romance catapults them into sublimity, beyond or "outside humanity," a state that Forster likens to the elements, to clouds, stenches, roars. Still not having sex, they nevertheless reach a state of exaltation in the pastoral setting, an anticipation of the life Maurice and Alec more promisingly pursue in the greenwood.

For his insurrection, Maurice is "sent down" by the dean and made to return home. Clive is not punished due to his exemplary status as his cohort's most accomplished classics scholar. Dean Cornwallis is no fool, rightly suspecting a budding romance and only too happy to nip it in the bud. Besides, he feels it is "unnatural" for men of distinct social classes, such as the highborn Durham and the middle-class Hall, to commingle (79–80). Back at home with his worried mother and somewhat acid-tongued sisters (Kitty chastises their mother for making Maurice feel important by worrying over him), Maurice relishes the exaltation less than he grimaces at his and Clive's lost opportunities. They had "only been together one day! And they had spent it careening about like fools" (82). They correspond with one another, each saying "I love you," but the letters, far from satiating them, cause discomfort, which they confess to one another during a dreary lunch in town (83).

In a scene reproduced in the film, Maurice is castigated by Dr Barry for his ill treatment of his mother once he has been sent down (the film adds Mrs Hall and his sisters listening outside and his mother wincing at Maurice's stern talking-to). Dr Barry maintains the position that when a woman calls upon him for aid, as the distraught and bewildered Mrs Hall has done when faced with Maurice's obnoxious truancy, he will fulfill his obligations entirely. In contrast, unapologetic Maurice is a "disgrace to chivalry."

Interestingly, Maurice interprets Dr Barry's opprobrium through the lens of heterosexual privilege. "If a woman had been in that side-car, if then he had refused to stop at the Dean's bidding, would Dr Barry have required an apology from him?" (85). Mentally torpid though he is, Maurice finds a critical sensibility through his same-sex attractions, which put him at a remove from traditional heterosexual rituals and norms. He can see through the normalizing conventionality that dictates Dr Barry's attitudes. Still, Maurice is indeed a cad for treating the women in his life so horribly, for which he deserves censure.

Middle-class Maurice finally visits Clive at his family's ancestral country estate, Penge, impressive but decaying. "Maurice, I shall kiss you," Clive announces when he visits Maurice in his guest room. Clive sits on his friend's shoulder, presumably as they both lie on the bed in Maurice's guest room (the film blocks the scene this way). In one of his customary class-based observations, Forster has Clive retain his physical proximity to Maurice without the slightest nervous alteration when a housemaid bearing hot water enters the room. We know this is a notable bit of information because "Maurice started" when the housemaid knocked at the door, but Clive indifferently shouts, "Come in!" Maurice would have shifted position so that the housemaid would not see his and Clive's bodies in intimate connection, whereas Clive could not care less that the housemaid sees them this way. For his part, Maurice acutely monitors the ways that Penge receives him, wondering if the far-away location of his accommodations indicates a slight. But it seems the room's location indicates Clive's plans for exclusivity, giving them the chance to avoid anyone else: "Except for meals we need never be in the other part of the house," he reassures his friend (88).

After dinner, Maurice and Clive, finally alone and in the study, speak contentedly, enjoying their exclusive company. Clive, tapping his heart with his pipe, explains to Maurice that he has touched him deeply. Maurice, childlike in his eagerness, asks Clive what it is about him that made Clive care for him. Some hedging follows, but then Clive says that if Maurice really must know, "Well, it was your beauty."

Maurice, who always seems surprised to hear such things, responds, "My what?" And he returns the high regard, telling Clive that he thinks he is beautiful as well, that he loves his "voice and everything to do with you." These panegyrics make Clive uncomfortable. The "folly" drains out of him, and he becomes serious and disciplining. Like a wiser, improvement-seeking guide, he tells his charge, "You've done all right, Maurice." And then his thoughts veer toward intellectual matters: "the precise influence of Desire upon our aesthetic judgments" (92).

When Maurice asks Clive if he will kiss him, Clive shakes his head no while both smile at one another, "having established perfection in their lives" (93). Clive's Platonic ideal when it comes to matters of sex – his ceaseless holding at bay of the sexual body, specifically his own from Maurice – would appear to be derived from the teachings of the German art historian Johann Joachim Winckelmann (1717–1768), a powerful influence on nineteenth-century homo-Hellenism. Discussing ancient sculpture, chiselled and alluring bodies on display, Winckelmann offers a plan for their proper contemplation: sexual desire must be sublimated (as Sigmund Freud theorizes was the case for the homosexual genius Leonardo da Vinci), the beautiful sexlessly appreciated.

Clive's formidable, steely mother (a memorable personage in the movie, played by Judy Parfitt) takes a walk with Maurice, whom she likes because, despite their class differences, he is no sycophant. At one point, she asks him if there is a woman in his life. When he and Clive are alone, they discuss reproductive futures. "These children will be a nuisance," Clive comments, referring to the expectation that he must produce an heir for Penge. Maurice advises that Clive just let himself keep "growing old," which Clive asks him to explain. Irritated but also immensely sad, Maurice contemplates "sterility" as a curse inflicted on homosexuals and others who defy Nature. At this point in the narrative, Clive continues to protest the sex and gender status quo: "Why children?" It's far more beautiful for "love to end where it begins" (96–7).

Things continue apace for two years. Encouraged by Clive to eat crow with Cornwallis, Maurice returns to Cambridge; he and Clive complete their degrees, then travel to Italy. Many opportunities for clandestine eros arise, but they abstain "from avowals ('we have said everything') and almost from caresses." Their relationship is passionately loving yet "temperate," adhering to the celibate Winckelmannian ideal (98).

When the men's families begin forming bonds of their own, drawn together without knowledge of the men's romantic ardour, Maurice and Clive find the whole thing amusing and irritating in equal measure. Fascinatingly, Forster makes explicit what we suspect of them all along: "Both were misogynists, Clive especially" (100). Clive's sister begins probing more sharply about his marital plans, while Maurice's family – always intimidated by him – do not. Hiding in plain sight, Maurice and Clive spend Wednesdays, an inviolable schedule, and possibly weekends together.

Clive passes his bar exams, securing plans of becoming a barrister, but also gets a slight case of influenza, which he passes on to Maurice. Visiting the Halls, Clive, still suffering illness's aftereffects, collapses. In a startling moment, Maurice, alarmed and attentive, kisses Clive, prostrate on the ground, in full view of his mother. Mrs Hall appears not to think anything of it since she readily accedes to Maurice's request that she not mention it to the others: "As you know, we are great friends, relations almost" (104–5).

Awkwardness arises when Maurice tries to dismiss the night nurse, making her way to the Halls' home, explaining to Clive that he can do a better job of looking after him. Clive, however, wants the nurse. When talking to his sister Ada about the situation, Maurice reveals his jealousy. When Ada reports that their mother wants Ada, not Maurice, to let the nurse in, for respectability's sake, Maurice emits one of his sarcastic, bitter little laughs that his sisters dislike so much. "At the bottom of their hearts they disliked him entirely, but were too confused mentally to know this"; hating his laugh provides the only vent (108).

Clive, recovering, decides that he must go to Greece, whereas Maurice has "no use for Greece" (110). Perhaps Maurice should have joined Clive's grand tour. It proves a decisive experience for Clive, who realizes that he no longer wants a romantic relationship, however Platonic, with Maurice. Clive sits in the theatre of Dionysius, contemplating their relationship, seeing "only dying light and a dead land." He has written his lover to say, "Against my will I have become normal. I cannot help it" (116). Maurice urges him, in a letter, to return soon and test out his resolve. But Clive has become resolute, tearing up the letter because he has "stopped loving Maurice" (117). Does Forster place Clive in the theatre of Dionysius – hardly an incidental venue, the cradle of classical Greek theater, where all its plays were performed – to suggest that everything Durham does from this point is a performance? Especially his performance as heterosexual male?

As we will discuss, the filmmakers found Clive's straight conversion unconvincing. To motivate it, they expanded Risley's role as an Oscar Wilde type, making him the target of a homosexual sting operation with a male prostitute, then "leniently" sentenced to six months' hard labour, and losing his political career. While the film's invention of much more concrete motivations for Clive's straight turn work well cinematically, there is something to be said for Forster's decision to leave this turn ambiguous. *Clive* himself is ambiguous, an enigmatic character throughout, which lends his sudden heterosexual shift an emotional consistency that does not require explication.[4]

Forster invites us to speculate. Perhaps Clive truly upholds the Hellenic-homo-aesthetic that embraces male homosexuality as a beautiful ideal while eschewing the body and sexual passion. Clive wants passion only in "temperate" form. As Forster clarifies, Clive feels nothing in the way of sexual desire for the woman he marries. His turn to heterosexuality, as the commentary in chapter 24 suggests, consists largely in wanting to be in the know, part of the larger order of things.

He is charmed by the nurse at his sickbed, and experiences it as a refreshing change when women respond to his appraising looks. Men never have: "they did not assume he admired them, and were either unconscious or puzzled" when they registered his probing gaze.[5]

Women, however, "took admiration for granted." Clive enjoys their knowingness, whether interested in him or not, the ways they welcome him "into a world of delicious interchange" (118–19). Perhaps Maurice's torpid reserve finally leaves privileged Clive too weary from the work of erotic intrigue; women promote these delightful sexually charged "interchanges" that flow so freely, no effort required.

In an extraordinary moment, Clive passes "a cinema palace," which he enters. "The film was unbearable artistically, but the man who made it, the men and the women who looked on – they knew, and he was one of them" (119). Cinema does not have to be any good artistically to wield an enormous influential and binding power. It reflects the image of heterosexual society back to itself, a glimmering mirror of its secure and orderly rightness and ease. The director or producer of the film, "the man who made it," knowingly establishes a partnership with the male and female spectators, who "know" exactly what is going on, too. Forster links the emergent technology and art form (emphasizing the former) of the cinema to heteronormative standards that bind men and women together through shared knowledge of its rituals and forms.

Clive experiences class-based revulsion when dining with the overheated Halls, finding their dinner and conversation equally humid. Ultimately, he faints. He weeps when Maurice kisses him because his love for Maurice has died. Clive now finds his devoted friend boring. This produces a response of "physical dislike" for Maurice that prefigures their "approaching catastrophe" (120). Maurice, who accepted a relationship without physical fulfilment in order to be with Clive, will be denied even this skimmed milk love affair.

Hoping to rehabilitate his friend with social engagements including women, to retain the friendship kernel after discarding the unwanted romantic shell, Clive pops over to the Halls one evening, and finds Kitty first (Maurice is still at work). Interestingly, Clive realizes how much he dislikes Kitty, who is as bored by Clive's stories of Greece as her brother would be but lacks Maurice's "gift of listening beneath words" (122). But then Ada and her mother come home, and Clive is struck by Ada's appeal, particularly that her and her brother's voices are "wonderfully alike" (123). Forster suggests that Clive can feel incipient passion for Ada because she reminds him of Maurice but is appropriately female. Indeed, Ada may not be the most seductive of women, but she embodies peace, calmly and reassuringly offering a "compromise between memory and desire" (124). This is an image of woman as tender helpmeet – an enduring nineteenth-century fantasy that helped soothe male fears.

Taking an ambulance class with Dr Barry, the sisters enjoin Clive in simulated first-aid scenarios, to which "Clive submitted his body to be bound" (123). (One cannot help remembering how much Maurice longs for such a submission.) When Maurice comes home and finds Clive bandaged up from head to foot, almost as if he has been ironically giftwrapped for the lover he will reject, Maurice can only say, "Why did you let them?" (126). When the men are alone, Maurice spars awkwardly, challenging Clive, "So you don't love me?" and insisting he'll have a row whether Clive wants one or not. Clive's nausea returns accompanied by the "horror of masculinity" that has put him off Maurice, whose threatened embrace makes Clive shudder.

The men continue to speak at cross-purposes. Maurice tries to convince Clive that he's "in a muddle," but Clive will have none of this, explaining that he has *changed*. To which Maurice, more provocative than previously, responds, "Can the leopard change his spots?" Anticipating his eventual rebellion against the heterosexist class order Clive represents, Maurice explains, "You and I are outlaws" (127).

When Maurice continues to insist that they belong together, that they love each other, Clive snaps, informing Maurice that if he were to love anyone at all, it would be Ada. Maurice, becoming hysterical, summons Ada, yelling for her. This behaviour appalls Clive, who insists that he will not stand for dragging a woman into their mess. Desperately angry, Maurice suddenly seizes upon Clive, bearing down on him and injuring him. The whole horrible exchange reduces Maurice to tears (129).

Maurice alarmingly shuts the door to the study and locks it. After concernedly (or simply "nervously") calling out to Maurice, and doing his best to reassure the summoned Ada, Clive decides to leave. As he ventures to the train station, he registers the sadness of his and Maurice's terminated friendship. He acknowledges Ada as a "transitional" object, someone he will not marry. But she signals a future possibility dawning just ahead, "some goddess of the new universe" awaiting him in London (130). So ends part 2.

Part 3 opens with one of the novel's most unpleasant scenes, paranoid Maurice grilling Ada about her supposed relationship with Clive. "He accused his sister of corrupting his friend." Maurice invents accusations from Clive about her licentious conduct. And when she heartbreakingly tries to defend herself and asks Maurice to reassure Clive that she meant no such thing, he spitefully responds that she's got "the satisfaction of breaking up that friendship." Ada sobs, saying, "you've always been unkind to us, always" (134).

Maurice glumly lives on in his half-dead way, going to work dutifully. But, however horribly he behaves to Ada, he is far unhappier than she, roaming in a vast open-ended loneliness. As he does so, he imagines possibilities. "He was an outlaw in disguise." "Two men can defy the world." He also begins to contemplate suicide (135). Maurice tells Clive these things in their ongoing letters while they maintain virtual relations.

Maurice dwells on suicide, coming home and handling a pistol while knowing he will not use it. His loneliness grows and expands and becomes his life. But there is some positive change. He apologizes to Ada once she becomes engaged to his old school chum Chapman. "Ada, I behaved so badly to you," he says (141). But Ada has been hurt by Maurice's treatment too deeply to forgive him. Moreover, she actually did feel the stirring of passion with Clive, and Maurice squelched that. She brusquely responds to his wishes for her happiness. What's more, his attempts to make amends with Kitty do not prove any more successful. Indeed, their mother notices his sisters' desultory attitude toward a brother they once respected, but Mrs Hall, fond of him though she is, will not fight for Maurice any more than she fought against him when he disrespected the dean. Maurice's listlessness signals the inescapable truth that his loneliness engulfs him (142–3).

Speaking of desultory: Maurice learns that Clive is to be married from his mother, whose friendship with Mrs Durham has continued and supplied her with this intelligence. Maurice does not even receive this message from his mother directly; instead, she announces it into the breakfast table air, and it is Ada who asks to whom. "Lady Anne Woods," Mrs Hall responds. "He met her in Greece." The daft Mrs Hall has misquoted Mrs Durham's letter, which runs, "I will now tell you the name of the lady: Anne Woods" (145). Maurice chafes against knowing Clive did not mention this to him.

In the meantime, the Halls are putting up Dr Barry's teenage nephew Dickie, and Maurice has succumbed to the young man's charms. Urged by his family to rouse the lad from bed where he slumbers after last night's dance, Maurice contemplates Dickie's sleeping form: "He lay with his limbs uncovered. He lay unashamed, embraced and penetrated by the sun. The lips were parted ... the body was a delicate amber. To anyone he would have seemed beautiful, and to Maurice who reached by two paths he became the World's desire" (146–7). Though an attractive man himself, Maurice at this point in his life stares at Dickie as if contemplating one of those rarefied human beings, like Hyacinth and Ganymede, who rouse the passions of gods. (Adding to his qualities, Dickie has "a graceful body beneath his clothes … a freshness … he might have arrived with the flowers" [148].)

Maurice's desire for young Dickie establishes that his love for Clive is only one manifestation of his homosexual desire, meaning that Maurice is ready for more. Unfortunately for him, Dickie shows no interest and ignores Maurice's heavy-handed sexual hints. (The film originally included this subplot but cut it from the final version. It is included in the deleted scenes on the Cohen Media Blu-ray.)

Forster makes explicit the non-sexual nature of Maurice and Clive's relationship, and reveals what his feverish contemplation of supine Dickie indicates: "Lust." Maurice stands vigilant against precisely the love that will eventually liberate him, the "feeling that can impel a gentleman towards a person of lower class." But Maurice gains, frustrated and deprived though he is, clarity: "it was not Clive who would heal him" (151–2). Clive eventually calls Maurice to tell him the news of his nuptials to his fiancée Anne.

In a most unpleasant episode, Maurice expresses his internalized homophobia by punching an old man in the face when he makes advances toward Maurice on a train. Forster renders the whole scene a pitiable one, emphasizing that the man "was elderly" and that his "nose streamed with blood over the cushions." Meanwhile, lust for young men rages in Maurice's heart; he cannot "keep away from their images" (155).

This chapter concludes with Maurice desperately seeking Dr Barry's help with his affliction. After a physical examination, Dr Barry pronounces him a "clean man," but Maurice remains miserable and gropes toward disclosure: "I'm an unspeakable of the Oscar Wilde sort." Dr Barry is predictably horrified and adamant. He refuses to hear another word about this and asks Maurice, "Who put that lie into your head?" (158–9). No talking cure for Maurice, and Dr Barry maintains the middlebrow silence that kills Maurice's soul.

Maurice, stumbling in the "Valley of the Shadow of Life" (22), comes to wonder, in an extension of the metaphor, if Risley, "capering at the summit" (34), might help him. And Risley eventually does, twofold. Bumping into Risley at a Tchaikovsky concert after his unproductive meeting with Dr Barry, Maurice learns from his Wildean old school chum that Tchaikovsky had dedicated the concert they just heard, "Symphonie Incestueuse et Pathique," to his nephew, with whom the composer had fallen in love. Maurice brushes off this knowledge and newfound "confidante" Risley both. But Maurice takes out a life of the composer from the library and discovers in it the one book he has read that has been of help to him. "'Bob,' the wonderful nephew," becomes the object of the composer's desire after the "disaster" of his marriage, the narrowly avoided fate prescribed to Maurice by Dr Barry.

Maurice resumes his abandoned childhood practice of masturbation. But it offers fleeting comfort. Risley once again comes to the rescue, having mentioned hypnosis with a knowing air. Strangely, he uses Dean Cornwallis as an example of someone with a related problem who has benefitted from hypnosis. Cornwallis's hypnotist coaches him, "You are no eunuch!" So, the dean that chastised Maurice for his joyride with Clive suffers from similar longings. Maurice bristles against Risley's knowingness, but gets his hypnotist's address from him anyway.[6]

Maurice finally gets the help he needs, even if it is from early twentieth-century conversion therapy – to which, thankfully, he does not succumb (162). Clive wants to help Maurice because he helped him endure the "three barren years before Anne" had "lifted him out of aestheticism into the sun and wind of love" (163). All this conciliation depends on Maurice keeping himself restrained and emotionless, reassuring Clive that no strange fits of passion will further intrude.

Clive and Anne maintain a respectful, tender, passionless rapport. Their sexual relations are perfunctory, permissible only because they are married. Men and women can have sex because nature approves, but one should not discuss it or extol it. And obviously sex between men is "inexcusable" (165).

Maurice takes a late-summer holiday at Penge, brooding over whether to see Risley's (Cornwallis's?) hypnotist, right before the Park v. Village cricket match. This is the visit where Maurice makes his reprehensible comments about the poor to Anne. Without yet knowing Alec Scudder by name, Maurice sees him "dallying with two of the maids," a flash of envy colouring the sight of the lustful gamekeeper. Maurice beholds in Alec and the "giggling" girls the image of frolicsome pleasure the world over. Free indirect discourse mingles the narrator's thoughts and Maurice's own. Shouldn't Maurice just "toe the line," take the normal sexual route? But Maurice, however improbably, holds out hope for "something from Clive" (166). (The film's deleted scenes on the Blu-ray include the one where Maurice catches sight of Alec, Milly the maid, and her cousin being physically flirtatious.)

In the morning Maurice and Clive's brother-in-law Archie London go out shooting rabbits on the grounds, sometimes settling for ferrets, which they miss. Alec is a largely invisible presence here, mentioning only that it was the men's fault they missed the ferret, as the guest reports to Maurice. (The film emphasizes Alec's brooding gamekeeper presence keeping time and bagging rabbits and fixating intently on Mr Hall.) Meanwhile, Maurice privately nurses a thrill: Mr Lasker Jones, the miracle-cure hypnotist, has wired him (173).

Anticipating, or desperately hoping, for conversion-therapy success from the hypnotist, Maurice tells Clive that he is hoping to get married, news that Clive wholeheartedly supports: "Maurice, I'm awfully glad. It's the greatest thing in the world, perhaps the only one" (174). Maurice responds to all this heterosexual boosterism with a brutality lost on the relieved, beaming Clive, who notes that the extraordinary Anne has already guessed Maurice's attachment. One wonders what Anne, gentle and gracious and charitable if privately self-interested, would make of the true nature of Maurice's present attachment, that he and her husband loved each other once, and that Maurice loves him still.

The chapter closes with Clive, emboldened by Maurice's seeming embrace of normal life and sex with women, establishing that he has not forgotten their prior intimacies. To demonstrate that he feels warmly toward Maurice and honours their past, he kisses his hand, which makes Maurice "shudder" (175). Before he departs Maurice's room, Clive holds out his hand for Maurice to kiss. Perfunctorily, Maurice "applied his lips to the starched cuff of a dress shirt" (176).

Meanwhile, Maurice and Alec do not instantly hit it off. Maurice complains to Archie London about Scudder's having refused to take the tip he offered him. "Damned cheek!" (177). When Alec wakes Maurice up, it will not be only sexually, but to the humanity of those of a lower-class status.

Maurice makes his way from Penge to his London appointment with Mr Lasker Jones, who informs him that he suffers from "congenital homosexuality," and that 75 per cent of his clients are like Maurice. Lasker Jones levels with his patient: he has only been successful in curing 50 per cent of his clients. The hypnotist begins his conversion work, getting the hypnotized Maurice to believe that he sees a picture on the wall and can perform feats such as jumping over a crack in the carpet, and asking his patient if he can see the lovely Miss Edna May. Both men chuckle at Maurice's remark, "I want to go home to my mother." When Maurice says of Miss Edna May that she does not attract him, the hypnotist chides him for being "ungallant." He urges Maurice to contemplate her "lovely hair," to which Maurice tearfully responds, "I like short hair best." When asked why, he answers, "Because I can stroke it" (182).

It is agreed that Maurice will return to Penge, described, fascinatingly, as "an emetic." More fascinating still, the "old poisonous life" that it purges consists of what had "seemed so sweet"; Penge cures "him of tenderness and humanity." I can think of no better critique of conversion therapy than this description of Penge and its ruling inhabitants, the model of the bourgeoisie, as an extension and reinforcement of Lasker Jones's practice (183).

In a subtly erotic passage, Maurice walks the grounds at night, as he enjoys doing, and the evening primroses stir "him by their odours." The detail that Clive "showed him evening primroses," but never "told him they smelt" begins a chain of floral sexual metaphors that now herald Alec's sudden appearance.

He apologizes in his formal yet ever so slightly cheeky way, for not having given Mr Hall and Mr London "full satisfaction." "That's all right, Scudder," Maurice responds, but is then taken aback when the gamekeeper adds, "Glad to see you down again so soon, sir," which Maurice finds a "subtly unsuitable" comment (184–5). Maurice has yet no inkling of just how deliciously unsuitable Alec's behaviour will turn out to be.

In rather a melancholy image, Maurice later that night has dinner with Mrs Durham (Clive's mother) and the rector Mr Borenius, who fusses over Scudder's soul. Alec has made plans, coordinated by his older brother Fred, to emigrate to Argentina. Eager to make sure that this licentious young man prone to corrupt housemaids will be confirmed in the Argentine, the rector gets into a religious argument with the atheist and bluntly skeptical Maurice, who once again demonstrates a surprising kinship with the working classes. Maurice moodily walks about the nighttime grounds. Natural odours again herald Alec's appearance, suffusing the air with delicate fruit scents that suggest "he has stolen an apricot" (190). One cannot help thinking of the James Ivory–adapted Luca Guadagnino film *Call Me by Your Name*, with its illicit apricots and, especially, peaches. Alec asks Maurice regarding Argentina, "Have you visited it yourself, sir?" Maurice affirms that it's only ever going to be "England for me" (190).

The film version, as we will see, breaks this action up into two scenes, but in the novel the restless Maurice, dreaming about hypnosis-implanted heterosexual scenes, suddenly wakes up, goes to the window, opens the curtains, sticks his head out into the cold, misty night air, and yells, "Come!" Shivering, he wonders why he did that and goes back to bed. No sooner does he do so than Alec has climbed the workmen's ladder outside Maurice's room and entered his room. Kneeling by Maurice's bed, the gamekeeper says, "Sir, was you calling for me? Sir, I know … I know," and begins touching the stunned but receptive virgin (192). So ends part 3.

Part 4, the novel's last section, opens with the deeply lovely and funny and touching scene of Maurice and Alec in bed. "Sir, the church has gone four, you'll have to release me," Alec tells his ardent captor (196). Asking Alec what his first name is, Maurice tells Alec to call Maurice by his. Call me by my name.

Gay liberation theory of the 1970s held that gay love and sex was a radical reordering of society, disrupting familiar and binding class, social, and racial difference. Forster's depiction of Maurice and Alec, inspired by the real-life love affair of Edward Carpenter and George Merrill, presages this revolutionary thought. Awaking "deep in each other's arms," Maurice and Alec enjoy a class-defying intimacy that inspires Maurice's Carpenterian, Whitmanian "Love of Comrades." He tenderly asks Alec, "Did you ever dream you'd a friend, Alec? Nothing else but just 'my friend,' he trying to help you and you him. A friend … Someone to last your whole life and you his. I suppose such a thing can't really happen outside sleep." The audacity of this novel is that it can happen; it does happen. But there will still be some work getting there. As departing Alec approaches the window to descend the ladder, Maurice calls out "Scudder" and the young man "turned like a well-trained dog." Class barriers will be among those that keep the new lovers apart. Still, Maurice's parting line to Alec in this scene is sweet-souled as can be, and rightly returns them to a first-name basis: "Alec, you're a dear fellow and we've been very happy" (197).

The cricket scene in chapter 39 has been much discussed. Maurice and Alec play on the same team, a team themselves on full public display only hours after they have first made love. Forster's description of their unity demands quotation: "They played for the sake of each other and their fragile relationship – if one fell the other would follow. They intended no harm to the world, but so long as it attacked they must punish, they must stand wary, then hit with full strength, they must show that when two are gathered together majorities shall not triumph. And as the game proceeded it connected with the night, and interpreted it" (201). Clive's cloddish entrance into the game brings it to a stop.

Forster provides a manifesto for transgressive same-sex love, a defiant follow-up to and extension of Maurice's fantasy of lifelong friendship. Nevertheless, Maurice and Alec immediately face impediments. Maurice grows wary of Alec's passionate efforts to arrange their subsequent tryst at the boathouse where the servant had initially asked if Maurice would bathe between cricket innings. Alec's wholly sincere and sexy letter to Maurice does not have the desired effect. Alec writes, "Dear Sir, let me share with you once before leaving Old England if it is not asking too much. I have key, will let you in" (207). Unfortunately, Maurice just feels panicked and guilty, and becomes convinced that Alec is trying to trap and blackmail him, most likely with an accomplice. He hastily makes another appointment with Mr Lasker Jones.

Mr Lasker Jones, ostensibly a quack doctor, is one of the most surprising characters in the novel. On his return visit, Maurice fails to be as suggestible as he was before. The hypnotist quickly detects the problem – Maurice is a leopard who won't be changing his spots. He advises his client to go to Italy or France, countries that have adopted the Napoleonic Code and no longer criminalize homosexuality. Remarkably humane advice, this, when Forster wrote this novel. Though psychoanalytic theory has had its complicated history with homosexuality and homophobia both, Lasker Jones makes a strong statement for the principled, nonhomophobic psychoanalytic stand of the kind that Freud took, saying, "as psychiatry prefers to put it, there has been, is, and always will be every conceivable type of person." He reminds Maurice that men of his kind were once put to death in England (211). And when Maurice, convinced he is being blackmailed, shows Alec's letter to the hypnotist, he remarks that he sees no menace in it. (He burns the letter as the unconverted Maurice looks on.)

Alec has his pride. Angry that Maurice has ignored him and left him coldly and singly presiding over the isolated boathouse, Alec writes Mr Hall again, this time threatening him directly. His threats and his longing and desire for Maurice coalesce: "You say, 'Alec, you are a dear fellow': but you do not write. *I know about you and Mr Durham.* Why do you say 'call me Maurice,' and then treat me so unfairly" (216)? Maurice has turned the pining Alec into the fearsome blackmailer.

Having been told by Alec where to meet him, or else, Maurice shows up at the British Museum on a rain-soaked Tuesday afternoon. Alec arrives dressed in his Argentina garb of "blue suit and bowler hat" (219). Their tense initial meeting is brought to a head by the sudden appearance of old Mr Ducie, who recognizes Maurice but cannot remember his name. Maurice in an oddly playful manner tells Ducie that his name is Scudder. All the while, Alec has been making threats, including the one that his formidable brother is waiting outside. The embattled men continue to spar, and at one point Maurice bluntly tells Alec that the law would be on Maurice's side: "the police always back my sort against yours" (225).

The ugliness between them is also a breaking apart of their defences and armour. Gradually, they find that they have begun to love one another consciously. Alec finally confesses he has not been serious about his blackmail threats; indeed, he growls, "I wouldn't hurt your little finger" (226). Alec convinces Maurice to break off a pressing work engagement, a formal dinner. It takes some convincing, but Maurice finally submits: "All right. To Hell with it" (227). They will share once more.

Waking up in the hotel room, Alec wants to keep canoodling. But Maurice twitches with anxiety – he wants to make plans. He encourages Alec to stay in England and to live with him. Alec, quite understandably, immediately balks at this idea even as he agrees with Maurice that they both love one another. "Stay? Miss my boat, are you daft? Of all the bloody rubbish I ever heard," Alec growls at him. Maurice is resolved, however, saying, "You can do anything once you know what it is" (231).

Maurice appears at the boat where Alec's family gathers to see him off to Argentina. Awkwardly standing with the Scudders and Mr Borenius, there with Alec's letter of introduction to an Anglican priest in Buenos Aires, Maurice could not be more out of place. Fred Scudder, Alec's brother, has none of his looks or charm, only his insolence and belligerence. Forlorn Maurice wants to capture his would-be lover's image in his mind. The sadness of this defeated scene saturates. But Alec continues to surprise Maurice, this time by not showing up to catch his boat. Maurice immediately realizes why – Alec has decided to abandon the Argentina plan and stay with him. With the achievement of love with Alec, Maurice, always in a torpor, gains a revolutionary clarity. "He knew what the call was, and what his answer must be. They must live outside class, without relations or money; they must work and stick to each other till death" (239). And that is what they both do.

Maurice reunites with Alec in the boathouse, who reveals that he'd sent Maurice a wire, telling him to come to the boathouse "without fail." This explains his sleepy but unruffled manner, reflecting his assumption that Maurice "got the wire." Alec covers them in glory when he utters his famous, chapter-concluding line, "And now we shan't be parted no more, and that's finished" (240).

Reconstructed as a person who renounces his class privilege to live an authentic desiring life with Alec, Maurice knows that his transformation demands one more phase. He must confront Clive. The film reverses this sequence of events: Maurice confronts Clive, then reunites with a sleepy but happily receptive Alec in the boathouse.

The last chapter focuses on this confrontation. Maurice catches Clive, just before he turns in for the night, to tell him about his love for Alec. Clive is aghast (242). Preternaturally calm, Maurice deflects Clive's series of protests and warnings and generally aghast response. He informs the man who kept his body inviolate that Alec has done the opposite. "I have shared with Alec," declares Maurice, using his lover's language. Clive, brazenly obtuse, asks, "Shared what?" To which Maurice responds, "All I have. Which includes my body" (243).

Clive's "whimper of disgust" is an interesting description as well as response (243). Why a whimper, and not, say, a bang of abuse? Is it possible that Clive still loves Maurice, in the way he promised he would? (This is the film's suggestion, as we will discuss.) When Maurice leaves, finally, never to be seen by Clive again, he leaves no trace save for "a little pile of the petals of the evening primrose" (246). The primrose had been associated with Alec and his scented air and sudden appearance, and now it is the emblem of and memorial to Maurice, a monument to which exists always in Clive's mind, even in old age, when Clive can still see his friend on the grounds of Cambridge, young as they both were then, "beckoning to him, clothed in the sun, and shaking out the scents and sounds of the May term" (246).

Chapter 3

The Boathouse:
Merchant Ivory's *Maurice*

Merchant Ivory was riding high. They had just scored their biggest success with *A Room with a View*, the movie that launched a thousand English majors and trips to Italy. Lucrative offers came their way as never before; a courtroom drama with Tom Cruise was in the works. But the team wanted to adapt E.M. Forster's novel *Maurice*, an immediately controversial choice. The reception that *Maurice* received when Forster's novel was finally published posthumously in 1971 was decidedly chilly and even derogatory, as we have discussed. Forster's literary executors at King's College, London, advised the team not to adapt *Maurice*: given the novel's purported inferiority, an adaptation of it would damage Forster's reputation. Ruth Prawer Jhabvala absented herself from the making of *Maurice* – she did, however, make significant contributions. Adding further tension was the fact that the film was made during the height of the AIDS crisis, a tragedy compounded by waves of homophobic response in the US and Britain. Margaret Thatcher's Section 28 made it illegal to mention homosexuality in schools, and US politicians and religious pundits such as Jerry Falwell and Pat Robertson framed AIDS as God's punishment on gays. Merchant Ivory's detractors viewed *Maurice* not only as further proof of the tone-deafness of the heritage film but also as a regressive throwback with little relevance to the real-world struggles of gays and lesbians. Given all these setbacks, it's a wonder that the movie was even made – and a boon to those of us whose lives have been indelibly touched by it.[1]

One of the criticisms of Merchant Ivory films landed with particular force on *Maurice*, given derision toward the source material: their adaptations were *too* faithful, too closely tethered to the works adapted for the screen. These concerns dovetail with problems inherent in the adaptation process. As Robert Emmet Long asks in *James Ivory in Conversation*, did Ivory and Jhabvala consciously strive to create a cinematic voice that resembles Forster's? Ivory responds: "Yes and no. His was a very pleasing voice, and it was easy to follow. Why turn his books into films unless you want to do that? But I suppose my voice was there, too. It was a kind of duet, you could say, and he provided the melody" (Long 2006, 200).

To call *Maurice* a faithful adaptation is both a fair judgment and a misleading one. For faithful almost always means "overly faithful," doctrinaire, paint-by-the-numbers, slavish.[2] It usually implies that the filmmakers have too simplistically and unimaginatively brought the source material to the screen, providing an illustration of literary action rather than probing analysis. Merchant Ivory is faithful to the source material in that there are no wild deviations from the original narrative, no characters altered beyond recognition or invented entirely anew. At the same time, it cannot be called a "hideous progeny," wildly distinct from its original source.[3]

Rather than faithful (or "hideous"), *Maurice* is an example of what I call *sympathetic adaptation*. Sympathetic adaptation views the source material favourably and honours its vision without being inextricably tethered to it. Sympathetic adaptation seeks not to reproduce the source material directly but instead to evoke, clarify, and heighten it. It thereby discovers its peculiar voice, allowing the adapter to articulate their view of the material.

Bringing *Maurice* to the Screen

In the gay publication the *Advocate*'s 1987 article on the making of the film, Ivory confessed to Marcia Pally, "I thought I could do the film quickly, before Ismail and I got committed to a Hollywood project. As it turned out, the writing and casting and filming were more complex than I thought. It took us 54 days to shoot, our longest shooting schedule ever." The film was funded by the British Channel Four and by the American Cinecom (Pally 1987, 109, 111).

Ivory emphasized that writing the script posed some difficulties. First, the "ending was sticky. The book leaves you with the impression that Alec and Maurice live happily ever after, but the book was written at the break of the First World War. A whole generation of boys was wiped out. Forster wrote an afterword on what might really happen to the young men in his novel, so we put in references to the upcoming war to give viewers a sense of it." Second, Clive Durham's "conversion" to heterosexuality needed a motivation not supplied by Forster. Ivory mentions that the novel makes this shift a believably gradual one, but "how were we to visualize this in film?" (Pally 1987, 53). Ivory underscores one of the difficulties of adaptation, not unique to his film: how to "visualize" literary character psychology, especially if it is elliptical, oblique, implicit.

Suzanne Speidel has written an invaluable study of Merchant Ivory's work-in-progress scripts, which the team donated to Forster's alma mater, King's College, Cambridge, adding to the college's archive the E.M. Forster Papers (Speidel 2014, 300). Of Merchant Ivory's three Forster adaptations, *Maurice* "contains the most radical changes across its draft screenplays" (Speidel 2014, 301).

Speidel's painstaking analysis contains several relevant points for us. "There are in fact four different versions of the *Maurice* screenplay" in the King's archives. Co-screenwriter Kit Hesketh-Harvey was at that point a staff producer for the BBC-TV Music and Arts Department. He was also the brother-in-law of Julian Sands, who played the heroine's love interest in *A Room with View* and was scheduled to star in the title role of *Maurice*. (Sands ended up bowing out of the project, due, according to Ivory, to "a general upheaval in his life. He left the film and ended up in California. An agent promised him a Hollywood career, no doubt" [Pally 1987, 110]. Given my admiration for Wilby's performance, I can only see this shift in casting as fortuitous, which is to take nothing away from Sands's golden charm in *A Room with a View*.)

Hesketh-Harvey had not previously written a screenplay, but he brought to the project an intimate familiarity with Forster's Cambridge milieu and society. "There is … no version of the screenplay that indicates which portions were written by Ivory and which by Hesketh-Harvey" (Speidel 2014, 304). "The great thing about Forster's dialogue," Hesketh-Harvey has observed, "is that it is written almost as screen dialogue. It is wonderfully precise" ("The Story of *Maurice*").

Perhaps the biggest revelation of Speidel's research is the extent to which Jhabvala, despite her vaunted non-involvement, contributed to the *Maurice* screenplay, its first draft especially. Speidel notes that the two Forster adaptations written by Jhabvala "are full of her own and Ivory's margin notes." "In the case of *Maurice*," however, "there are fewer margin notes overall and almost none by Hesketh-Harvey, though Ivory has annotated the manuscripts. The earliest of the manuscripts contains a large amount of additions and suggestions by Ruth Prawer Jhabvala, most of which were subsequently acted upon, either in the next two versions of screenplay or in the editing of the film" (Speidel 2014, 303).

Jhabvala's chief contribution, though far from her only one, was to "correct" an apparent lacuna in Forster's novel: Clive's turn to heterosexuality and rejection of Maurice. As Ivory has frequently indicated, a general sense existed that Forster's depiction of this turn, occurring during Clive's sojourn to Greece, was frustratingly unpersuasive. I argue that Forster makes it plausible, closely related to Clive's pragmatism and general indifference to sex, an act that he can perform functionally and passionlessly with his eventual wife. But the film opts for a much more direct motivation. The Cambridge dandy Risley, left unscathed in the novel as a Wildean wit, becomes a tragic Oscar Wilde figure in the film; caught in a homosexual sting operation at a pub after soliciting sex from a cavalryman in league with the police, he is publicly shamed and sentenced to six months in prison with hard labour. The film presents Risley's public humiliation as all the motivation Clive needs to become straight and marry a woman.

"The most crucial difference between the novel and the three screenplays in the King's archive (not including the post-production script, which effectively transcribes the film itself) concerns the chronology of the narrative." The "writers' experimentations with story chronology" include an initial structure containing "nine flashbacks ... fantasies within flashbacks ... flashbacks within flashback." In the totality of work-in-progress screenplays and the final script, "the number of flashbacks fluctuates from nine, to three, to eight, to two, to none," which suggests "something of a pack-shuffling element to the business of narrative chronology" (Speidel 2014, 303–5).

The complexity of these various script versions "makes clear that the writers' aim was to reshape radically how we witness Maurice's emotional and sexual development: whilst Maurice's trajectory still follows the pattern of 'love, loss, another love,' the Maurice we first meet in the treatment and screenplays is the older man who has already loved and lost Clive, though he has not yet loved and won Alec" (Speidel 2014, 306). The final film proceeds chronologically, adhering to the novel's structure of beginning with the child Maurice and ending with his passionate, relationship-affirming reunion with Alec and final conversation with Clive. The film reverses the order of these two last scenes: Maurice breaks the news of his romance with Alec to Clive and then reunites with Alec in the boathouse. The film concludes with a shot of Clive and Anne in their bedroom window after Clive has imagined seeing the handsome young Maurice during their university days. As Ivory explained, "we shot the film with a great chunk of the story in flashback ... When it came time to edit the film, we edited it according to this flashback structure. But it wasn't good. It was confusing. The flashback went on too long and, when it was over, you wondered where the hell you were. Ismail didn't like it at all" (Bram 1997).

Clive's memory-image of Maurice at the end of the film pays homage to the initial narrative and chronological experimentation on the part of the screenwriters. The initial flashback structure, though rejected, undoubtedly shapes the film we have, its sense of loss and fleeting, unrecapturable, or unfulfillable connections and fantasies. It seeps affectingly into the finished film, adding an aching resonance to scenes where Maurice's lonely, ardent longing for Clive, especially when he roams Greece as Maurice spends his time in London, adrift and hoping for some word or sign from his would-be lover, finds cinematic expression.

Several moments and at least two of Forster's characters ended up on the cutting-room floor. The Hall sisters' friend Gladys Olcott, at whom Maurice unsuccessfully makes a pass, and Dr Barry's teenage nephew Dickie, whom Maurice lusts over, were originally included in the film, but did not make the final cut. Their cut scenes and other moments form a sizable selection of deleted scenes that can be seen on the Cohen Media Blu-ray (2017). I will discuss the deleted scenes at the end of this chapter.

◆ ◆ ◆

Merchant Ivory films consistently demonstrate a genius for casting, which more than holds true for *Maurice*. James Wilby recalls, in the Blu-ray featurette "The Story of *Maurice*," that he "went for a general casting with Jim Ivory." Julian Sands had already been cast in the lead. Wilby remembers Ivory saying that he could not be cast due to his resemblance to Sands. When Sands left the film, surmises Wilby, Ivory went back to the similarly tall and blond Wilby. Julian Wadham was also considered for the lead and was subsequently cast as one of Maurice's fellow stockbrokers.

Wilby and Hugh Grant knew each other, having acted together in an Oxford University student feature film, the 1982 *Privileged*, directed by Michael Hoffman. Grant, still relatively unknown, not actively pursuing acting roles, and doing stand-up comedy at the time, was recommended by Hesketh-Harvey to Ivory: "Cast Hughie, he'll make us laugh." Wilby reports having contacted Grant when they were both auditioning for Ivory and getting together to rehearse the scenes in advance. Rupert Graves made his screen debut in the role of Freddy Honeychurch in *A Room with a View* – a performance he was unhappy with – and jumped at the chance to give a better one in *Maurice*. He clearly continued to appeal to Ivory (and his performance in *Room* remains charming, a pleasing anticipation of his complex performance in *Maurice*). Graves would act opposite Wilby again in the 1988 screen adaptation of Evelyn Waugh's *A Handful of Dust*, and join the cast of another Forster adaptation, not Merchant Ivory's, the 1991 *Where Angels Fear to Tread*.

Several British eminences are cast in key supporting roles: Ben Kingsley, Billie Whitelaw, Denholm Elliott, Judy Parfitt, Simon Callow, Barry Foster. All these performers make an indelible mark on the film, as does Mark Tandy as Risley and Patrick Godfrey as Simcox.

In our discussion of *The Bostonians*, we highlighted key aspects of Ivory's period film style, particularly the deliberately leisurely, lifelike pace, the lived-in quality of the surroundings, the offhand familiarity with the setting and its environment. Belén Vidal has outlined the cinematic components of Ivory's period filmmaking and their shaping contributions to the heritage film. She notes their "antiquarian reconstruction of the past that relies on the verisimilitude of the detail. The attention to houses and their interiors (Ivory's own background is in architecture and fine arts) that characterizes the mise-en-scène of these films stresses the importance of location and atmosphere." Discussing the long take of Ruth Wilcox (Vanessa Redgrave) strolling on the grounds of the titular house in *Howards End*, Vidal links Mrs Wilcox's dreamy affect to Ivory's style, "the long takes and slow tracking movements," the "languid" pace and the evocation of a "lost era," "the expansive widescreen frame" and "deep-focus, horizontal compositions." She observes that "the affective meanings of the film are deeply intertwined with the textures of the mise-en- scène, and with the figuration of time," and adds that "the feeling of 'at-home-ness' in the past as a construct of imagination" figures the past as "the 'other' of the present in terms of the affective duration of memory" (Vidal 2012b, 72–5). As I will have frequent opportunities to show, *Maurice* anticipates *Howards End* in its treatment of time, pastness, futurity, and the liminal presence of and interaction between temporal modes. Which is to repeat, the

Figure 15
Behind the scenes during the making of *Maurice*.
www.merchantivory.com/film/maurice.

film benefits from and retains the residues of the flashback-driven structure of the early screenplays.

The film opens with a widescreen shot of a bearded and bespectacled man – Maurice's prep-school teacher Mr Ducie (Simon Callow) – leading a group of male schoolchildren across the grassy clifftop of a beach one windblown afternoon. What appears to be a father and his two sons fly kites as the party makes their way past them, the father nodding courteously to Ducie, as if affirming the self-appointed fatherly role he will soon take with one student. This long shot of Ducie and the young males frames the ritual as archetypal and subtly establishes the film's preoccupation with male group identity, from which Maurice and the schoolmaster literally break away. Ducie suddenly takes the adolescent Maurice (Orlando Wells) aside, the schoolboys walking in the opposite direction. As they proceed toward the shore, the schoolmaster asks the boy questions that confirm he has no father or brothers, no males at all in his life.

We do not learn, as we do in Forster's novel, that Ducie has decided to single out Maurice for special instruction – the "good talk" – the content of which his colleagues know already. Rather, there is a kind of thrownness – we leave the other boys behind and stroll alongside Ducie and Maurice. In this manner, we are made to identify with Maurice, not knowing what to expect, leaving behind his peers, and following the older man.

Ducie's good talk concerns the subject of heterosexual intercourse, which he describes as the physical side of the far more important spiritual bond between man and woman. Implicitly, Ducie has singled Maurice out for sex instruction because the boy needs to hear it.

The longstanding view of Merchant Ivory films as "phlegmatic" adaptations (Pauline Kael's term) proceeds in ignorance of one of the defining aspects of their work: their comic sensibility (Kael 1989, 359). Ducie's sexual instruction is depicted as a comic episode, albeit with an undertow of melancholy, that combination also being typically Merchant Ivory.

Figure 16
Maurice's sex education at Mr Ducie's hand.

First, casting the hirsute, plummy-voiced Simon Callow, who always seems too much of something (here, too sincere, too hairy, too plummy, too English), as Ducie lends the schoolmaster a disarming silliness. Though dressed in scholarly tweeds, the overemphatic, theatrical Ducie suggests something of a carnival performer, the "Professor" of spells and forbidden lore, reinforced by his umbrella used as a drawing implement. Wielding this stylus, Ducie etches anatomical drawings of male and female reproductive organs in the sand. Bearing a recognizable but denatured relationship to life, these drawings evoke a strange and mysterious language. Or, from certain angles, the abstract-genital visual art of H.R. Giger, who inspired the *Alien* films.

All the while, plummy-voiced Callow/Ducie announces the name and purpose of each drawn figure in Latin, lending the whole scene a pomp and silliness, the latter quality stemming from Ducie's lack of awareness of how the-atrical he sounds. Stabbing the sand with his long implement, Ducie gives the Latin name for each of his creations, pronouncing the V's as W's (*"membrum virile; wajina"*). The Latin terms are added by the adaptation, not being present in Forster's novel. The schoolmaster's Latin pronunciation and terminology are at times incorrect, quietly undermining the heavy-handed lessons.[4] Does Ducie fumble in his Latin pronunciation out of nervousness or ignorance? Whatever the case may be, it adds to the comic effect.

Ducie frames his lesson as being centrally about "the sacred mystery of sex … the act of procreation between husband and wife." Ostensibly, he explains the mechanics of heterosexual intercourse to Maurice, yet his explanation de-pends on euphemism. For example, to describe penetration, he begins, "Then, the man lies very close to the woman," and outlines the process that eventually leads to the birth of a child. It's all quite overbearing and funny.

Perhaps it is no surprise, then, that the fourteen-year-old object of his in-struction responds with ambivalence. As he does in the novel, the adolescent Maurice, played affectingly by Wells, after hearing all this lavish instruction, says, simply and bluntly, "I think … I *shan't* marry." Ducie pooh-poohs Mau-rice's dissenting remark, saying that he and his wife will ten years to the day receive Maurice and his wife for dinner at the schoolmaster's home, to which the boy responds with suitable solemnity ("Oh, *sir!*").

The film includes a comic moment from the novel and adds one of its own. Ducie and Maurice, still on the shore, attempt to catch up with the rest of their party when Ducie suddenly remembers the drawings on the sand and panics that they might be seen by the party of ladies accompanied by an older male now approaching the spot. Maurice reassures his schoolmaster that the tide will erase them. Then, we cut to a shot of a young girl, having walked ahead of her party, staring down at the sand etchings. When the older women catch up to her and look down at the drawings, one of them – presumably her mother – suddenly convulses in disgust, grabbing her daughter and mov-ing her away from the obscene tableau: "Come, Victoria!"

The young girl is the chief interest of this scene. As she gazes down at the sand drawings, her expression betrays neither confusion nor horror. If anything, she looks serenely untroubled. Her female guardians express a dismay that she never exhibits. And that the girl is called "Victoria" can be no accident. The line "Come, Victoria" allegorizes Victorian England's repressive attitudes toward sexuality, the basis for Freud's theories; the women jerking the child away from the scene of sex represent the guardians of morality and the sexual order. But if Young Maurice decides he shan't marry, Young Victoria looks at the evidence with an unclouded, unneurotic curiosity. Both children, then, align in their resistance to the expected gendered conduct foisted upon and demanded from them.

The shots of the schoolfellows walking on the beach are naturalistic, as are the shots of Victoria and her guardians making their way down to the shore. But Ducie and Maurice walk along the beach in long shots that bring this prefatory section to a close. The effect of these distanced views, the surging water and afternoon sky beyond them, suggest something more elemental and supernal, appropriate for the momentousness of occasion.

The next section of the film takes a considerable leap. We are at Cambridge University during Michaelmas term (fall term, from September or October to Christmas) in the year 1909 and in Dean Cornwallis's (Barry Foster) room. Maurice, now an adult male and university student, dines with his classmates and the dean. The camera pans from a view of the courtyard in the late afternoon light visible through the windows of the dean's room and then into the room itself, where Maurice and his classmates eat dinner and argue over music, the dean seated on the sofa on the far right, Maurice seated tensely on the sofa opposite him.

Maurice's friend Chapman (Mark Payton) makes philistine remarks about the silliness of opera, while Risley (Mark Tandy) defends music as the highest form of the arts. Risley stands while others remain seated, then moves about and commands attention with his height, bearing, stature, and precise, modulated, airy elocution. (Mark Tandy's pronounced widow's peak lends Risley a distinctive appearance to match his personality.)

All the while, the dean makes deflating remarks to the Wildean Risley and encourages Chapman and Maurice to take more helpings. Maurice remains tensely focused on his meal. Risley sits next to him after Maurice dares to enter the lofty discussion. Maurice takes his usual conservative view, advising Risley to keep his high-culture ideas to himself. Risley's position on the sofa next to Maurice is louche and suggestive, matching his self-important and insinuating aplomb.

Coming out of the building after the dean's meal, Maurice and Chapman are suddenly overtaken by Risley, who suggestively – every action of his can be described this way – invites Maurice to his rooms in the famously exclusive Trinity College. He adds that he knows people Maurice will find interesting. Is this, to put it anachronistically, Risley's gaydar at work, especially considering that Maurice gave no outward indication of kinship with Risley? Referring to Chapman, Risley advises, "No reason to bring your friend." What is intriguing to imagine is the narrative that does not enfold, a Maurice-Risley relationship. This does not enfold because when Maurice does venture to Risley's rooms later that evening, he finds not Risley but Clive.

James Ivory is one of the cinema's great visual stylists. Trained early in the fine arts, he brings a painterly eye to his images. Here is a case in point. To convey the significance of Maurice's life-changing visit to Risley – and to indicate that Maurice has hidden depths since he accepts the invitation of someone towards whom he seemed so hostile – Ivory and the cinematographer Pierre Lhomme devise one of the most beautiful and mysterious shots in the Merchant Ivory archive. Maurice, gowned, nervous, and extrovert, practices what he will say to Risley before he does so. It is early evening, dark with some faint light left. In long shot, with Maurice at the opposite end, we watch our hero make his way toward us in the cloistered walkway beneath the main room of the Wren Library in Trinity College's Nevile's Court.

The pillars flanking Maurice on either side lend the image a sombre classicism that ironically highlights the insecurities Maurice vividly exhibits. He practices his opening remarks to Risley, variations of "Salutations, Risley! You've bargained for more than you've gained." Maurice has moved to the foreground of the shot, and at the other end, where Maurice had once stood, a group of students walks by and snorts derisively at Maurice's plaintive fumbling.

This shot is so overpoweringly beautiful that it looks *created*, a matte shot, and threatens to overwhelm the action being depicted. But that it does not do so is itself testament to Ivory's visual genius and his ability to match formal concerns to content. Here, the architectural beauty and grandeur of the cloisters, draped in shadow, lend the entire comic yet apprehensive scene a quiet and persistent urgency. The film began with Ducie's epithalamion, but now it marshals its aesthetic forces to give Maurice's imminent same-sex courtship its own aesthetic significance.

The shots establishing the Nevile's Court setting include a long shot of the Wren Library in its entirety, with sculptured figures at the top, standing above a fleet of stained-glass windows. As the embarrassed Maurice, ridiculed by passersby, makes his way out of the walkway, we then cut to a less distanced, low-angle shot of the sculpted figures above the Wren Library. Now, they look less like intimidating sentinels policing infractions against the decorum of the court and more like impelling Muses, promoting desire.

When Maurice enters Risley's room, Risley isn't there. Instead, we find Clive Durham, seated on the floor and surrounded by heaps of pianola records. Durham explains that he is reading a paper on Tchaikovsky and hunting for Risley's copy of the Pathetic Symphony. He remarks, "Fetherstonhaugh's got a Pianola," which Maurice affirms, identifying this student as his upstairs neighbour. Durham decides to go back with Maurice and avail himself of Fetherstonhaugh's pianola.

Durham's surprise appearance in Risley's room magically replaces Risley, a problematic object of desire, with Clive, a more suitable one. The image of

Clive – both an aristocrat and senior to Maurice – in the heaps of pianola records is disarming. That Clive sits on the floor surrounded by tubes of music, making a most unsophisticated first impression, puts him and his new-found, less wellborn acquaintance on a more equal footing. Durham speaks with a Risley-like intrigue when he says, surprised to hear that Maurice (of all people?) knows Risley, "He's a dangerous man." Clearly, if Durham isn't "out" to Risley, they share coded knowledge of one another's proclivities.

Ivory's blocking and the actors' performances suggestively evoke the closet and the possibilities of freeing oneself from it. Maurice, peeking his head into Risley's room, remains half-in, half-out. The sliver of his visible physical body sharply contrasts with the door's ponderous expanse. He becomes more vis-ible, just as his sexuality, barred from him, now gains accessibility. Maurice eventually succeeds in entering Risley's room. Ivory begins with medium shots of the men that lead to medium close-ups, conveying an almost subliminal growing intimacy and proximity.

I say almost subliminal to register the way Ivory's emotional effects some-times work, specifically the bond, erotically suffused, that grows between Mau-rice and Durham. As they depart Trinity College and make their way to Fetherstonhaugh's room, Durham insists on carrying a pile of pianola records, far too many for him to carry. Maurice offers to help, Clive demurs, and then Maurice says, simply but decisively, "Give," and grabs hold of several cum-bersome tubes. It's a same-sex version of the archetypal carrying-her-school-books-home gesture.

In the neighbouring student's room, Durham and then Maurice play Tchaikovsky on the pianola, Durham's version more accomplished and mea-sured, Maurice's more impulsive and rapid. All the while, Fetherstonhaugh, a haughty young bespectacled man who might be queer himself, sits in the background reading Sophocles and issuing the occasional retort. As Maurice begins playing at the pianola, Durham walks about the room, airily advising Fetherstonhaugh to read the Greek tragedian for the characters rather than the author ("It's much more fun"), picks up a piece of fruit, announces,

Figure 17
Clive guides Maurice at the pianola.

"Fetherstonhaugh, I think am going to eat one of your apples," takes a lusty
bite, walks over to the pianola and its player, and advises Maurice that he
needs to play more slowly. Somehow, by the time this scene is over, we realize
that Maurice has been eating from Durham's apple, because Durham takes it
back from him and gives it another chomp. And Durham instructs Maurice's
pianola-playing hands with his own. This is the behaviour of lovers at one
with each another, though the two men have only just met. Intimacy has occurred before our unsuspecting eyes and will develop swiftly from here.

◆ ◆ ◆

It's Lent Term, 1910, and we join Maurice and Durham in the former's room, the latter complaining about his enervating vacation and the rows he has had with his mother because she refuses to accept that he's not a Christian. "I despise her character," Durham remarks, adding, "I've told you something no one else in the world knows."

"Rotten vac, eh?" Maurice says softly, and affectionately cuffs Durham's head with a boxing-glove-clad hand. (As we will see, Maurice is adept at boxing and plays the sport with working-class men whom he instructs in the pugilist art.) "Yes, it was, pain and misery," Durham complains, which leads Maurice to tease him more aggressively with the mock punches: "Misery and hell, eh!" Rapidly, the men fall to the ground and Maurice begins wrapping Durham up in a rug, tickling him, too. "You must let me go!" Durham comically protests. His humorous command anticipates Alec Scudder's equally humorous but much more openly sensual plea, the morning after Maurice and the gamekeeper have made love for the first time, "Sir, you have to release me."

Maurice overturns a wicker garbage basket (a harmless punishment, since the basket contains only crumpled-up paper) on the immured, supine Clive's head. As he does so, with a mischievous glint in his eye, he says, "I know you think I don't think. But I can tell you I do." Wilby adds an antic quality to his line reading ("I can tell you I *dooo*") that conveys Maurice's growing desire to break out of constrictions (from Clive's perspective we look up at Maurice, straddling us). The novel makes it achingly clear that Maurice finds thinking a chore and strains toward insight. The movie conveys this by depicting Maurice's playfighting as clearly motivated by a desire to become closer to Durham but not yet a self-aware signal of sexual interest. Which is to say, the movie gives Maurice the time he needs to connect with and articulate his desires.

Perhaps the next scene gives us, however subtly, our first indication that Maurice is beginning to recognize the nature of his desire. In Dean Cornwallis's room, Maurice and his fellow students translate passages from ancient Greek into English, and from a highly significant text, Plato's *Phaedrus*, a dialogue famous for its theory of same-sex love and desire.

Figure 18
"Omit the reference to the unspeakable vice of the Greeks," the dean instructs.

This key scene commences with a shot of three pairs of men's shoe-clad feet. The camera rises to show us Maurice and two classmates sitting on one sofa, all dutifully following each student's passage translations. Across from Maurice sits his friend Chapman and another student; across from them are Cornwallis and Fetherstonhaugh. Maurice never translates out loud, but he does listen keenly.

The students translate the section of Plato's dialogue *The Phaedrus* that concerns the love of males for other males, "the stream of longing" that the god Zeus, inflamed with desire, felt for his handsome young cupbearer Ganymede, ravished by the god in the form of an eagle. Maurice's cheerful but uninteresting friend Chapman (the one to whom Risley did not extend an invitation) translates these lines: "Every human soul has, at some stage, beheld an excellent being. When the soul gazes upon the beauty of that being, its beloved, it is nurtured, and is warmed, and is glad." Maurice looks up from his book at the mention of the word "beloved."

Fetherstonhaugh continues the translation, discussing the growing intimacy between the lover and the beloved, established in part when the lover fondles his friend in "gymnasium," a line at which Chapman derisively snorts. The earnest Fetherstonhaugh continues, "the current, which Zeus in love with Ganymede, the stream of longing" – and here he is interrupted by Cornwallis, who delivers one of *Maurice's* most famous lines: "Omit the reference to the unspeakable vice of the Greeks." Barry Foster's finely modulated delivery imparts a suitable censoriousness. The beloved, the translating student continues, "is experiencing a counter-love, a reflection of the love he inspires, and he thinks of it as friendship, not love, though, like his lover, he feels a desire to see, to touch, to kiss him."

That these lines pique Maurice's interest is subtly conveyed by Wilby and Ivory. Maurice would appear to be unconsciously associating Plato's evocations of same-sex desire with his burgeoning feelings for Clive. But the feelings build slowly, steadily.

The next scene features tableaux that encapsulate what many seem eager to associate with Merchant Ivory – pretty and retro images redolent of the heritage film. Maurice, Durham, and Risley go punting in the famed River Cam, Durham seated at one end of the boat, Maurice propelling the boat with a pole at the other end, and Risley, in a sunhat and sunglasses, louchely lying between them.[5] Durham determinedly rebukes Cornwallis's censorious treatment of *The Phaedrus*. "The hypocrisy of the man. He ought to lose his fellowship." In a manner redolent of the Wildean-Paterian late-Victorian enshrinement of homosexual eros as the highest form of love, Durham extols the love of male beauty and the beauty of male friendship in ancient Greek society. Referencing sex between men, Durham says, "I'm not advocating that." (Grant's line reading emphasizes "not" and "that.") He clarifies: "a masculine love of physical beauty and of moral beauty ... and of the beauty of the thirst for human knowledge – you omit that and you've omitted the

Figure 19
Clive defends homo-Hellenism to Risley and Maurice.

mainstay of Athenian society." Percy Bysshe Shelley, squeamish though he was about penetrative intercourse between males, would agree with Clive, hence Shelley's unexpurgated translation of what he titled *The Banquet*.

"I am not advocating that": Durham speaks from the position toward Greek love that Winckelmann pioneered. The idealized beauty of the male body in sculpted form could be celebrated so long as sexual desire was sublimated, a point that Freud would analogously make in his case study of the homosexual genius Leonardo da Vinci, the exemplary model of the homosexual artist who sublimates his sexual desire and channels it instead into profound artistic creativity. Winckelmann provided Wilde, Pater, and now Durham with a model for appreciating and extolling the beauty of ancient Greece including its model of homosexual love. But desire pulls on the body, making distanced aesthetic contemplation difficult when the only means of sexual connection. Maurice will grow frustrated with Clive's Winckelmannian reticence. Anticipating this, Maurice disputes Clive's homo-Hellenism, arguing that mainstream Christian thought makes far more societal impact than Plato.

The blocking of this scene, as Ivory's does always, speaks volumes. Clive sits at the head of the boat, speechifying (forecasting his eventual political career); Risley, sunhat- and sunglasses-sporting, lies louchely supine, a day vampire basking in the decadent sensuality that will undergo censure; Maurice punts, his relative class position making him naturally the labourer, ferrying his betters. No surprise that Clive and Risley unite to mock Maurice for his championing of Christ doctrine – "You know: the Redemption. The Trinity." – sarcastically singing trinitarian hymns as Maurice feebly defends his adamant but underfelt convictions.

Clive's steady and subtle radicalization of Maurice continues when the latter cuts chapel to meet his friend outside. As Maurice, his guilty gait the physical analogy to a stage whisper, makes his way out of the chapel during evening services, the diegetic "Miserere mei, Deus," Psalm 51 sung and beautifully set to music by Gregorio Allegri, mournfully saturates the scene.

In this narrative, every element organically corresponds to the whole. The psalm's language speaks to the conflicts and changes marking Maurice's life. "Wash me thoroughly from mine iniquity, and cleanse me from my sin." "Purge me with hyssop, and I shall be clean: wash me, and I shall be whiter than snow." "Hide thy face from my sins, and blot out all mine iniquities." But also: "Behold, thou desirest truth in the inward parts: and in the hidden part thou shalt make me to know wisdom." Not in the Christian theological way, Maurice desires truth in the inward parts, and to *know* wisdom. Ivory visually allegorizes his protagonist's disposition by filming Maurice's surreptitious exit from chapel as a gradual movement from darkness to light.

Maurice chides Clive for making him cut chapel. Yet the next scene shows us Maurice – back at home on "vac," seated and avidly eating breakfast while his mildly disapproving mother (the great Billie Whitelaw, famous for her

Figure 20
Swayed by Clive's irresistible appeal, Maurice cuts chapel.

collaborations with Beckett) and his sisters loom above him, dressed in a
rather dapper navy robe that contrasts with their church attire – rudely informing his mother that he will no longer attend church. His unruffled sisters
Kitty (Kitty Aldridge) and Ada (the delightful Helena Michell), irritated with
their mother for fussing over their recalcitrant sibling, tug on her to join them
and head out for church. In what sounds like a proto–coming out speech,
Maurice informs his mother that there is no point in trying to persuade him
to attend church services: "It's the way I am." Clive has wrought an apostate.
Mrs Hall reminds Maurice that his father always went to church, to which
Maurice responds, "I'm nothing like my father," leading to Mrs Hall's aghast,
mild-voiced "Maurice, what a thing to say. You are the very image of your father." Interestingly, both Maurice and Clive are pointedly paterfamilias-free.

And the central authority figure in Alec Scudder's life is not his father (or mother) but instead his older brother Fred, who books him the trip to Argentina attached to a future job. We remember Mr Ducie making quite a point of young Maurice's lack of older male guidance. Taken together, the central males' backstories offer a composite story of the gay man as fatherless.

Mention of their neighbour Dr Barry (Denholm Elliott, who plays Julian Sands's father in *A Room with a View*) produces a delicious bit of comedy that showcases a side of Maurice we have rarely seen. When Mrs Hall mentions Dr Barry as the person who noticed Maurice's spitting-image resemblance to his dead father, Maurice deflects, pointing out that Dr Barry doesn't attend church either, leading Mrs Hall to correct her children with, "Dr Barry is a most clever man. And so is Mrs Barry." Before the women depart, Ada turns to Maurice and points out her mother's syntactical slip: "Imagine – Mrs Barry's being a man!" Maurice laughs at this as heartily as he eats his breakfast. This rare moment of bonding humour between Maurice and the sister he will treat so abominably makes us feel more hopeful for priggish but progressing Maurice.

We shift to "Summer Term, 1910" and to one of many moments in *Maurice* that ensure its status as queer film classic. In Maurice's room, he sits on a wicker chair. Seated on the floor beside him and resting his head against Maurice's thighs is Clive. "Have you been alright?" Maurice asks. Clive responds, "Have you?" Maurice answers, "No," to which Clive responds, "You wrote that you were." All the while the "Miserere mei, Deus" plays non-diegetically, imbuing the entire exchange with portentous intensity.

The camera remains fixed on Clive's beautiful face in closeup. His lips are parted, revealing his teeth, an anticipatory attitude accentuated by his questioning, expectant eyes. As if in answer, Maurice begins exploring Clive's hair with his fingers, focusing on the left temple. Maurice then leans forward and puts his head on Clive's own, his dark hair contrasting with Maurice's floppy blond locks. Clive's hand reaches upwards to stroke Maurice's neck. He then decisively looks up at Maurice and rises up to sit in his lap, facing him. The men verge on kissing one another – at least, Maurice seems about to kiss Clive, and it appears that Clive is about to kiss him back.

As famous as the men's "platonic roving hands" (Kael 1989, 360), the sounds of the chair creaking as Maurice leans forward to roam Clive's hair and press his body against his friend's distinctively evoke their tentative yet insistent eros. As Raymond Ang aptly describes of Merchant Ivory, "There's something of the iceberg theory in their best work, with even-tempered gentility giving way to volcanic emotions bubbling underneath the surface. That quality is present in the films' most indelible moments: in the way James Wilby gently caresses Hugh Grant's hair in *Maurice*, for example, the discordant creaking of his chair becoming a kind of metronome to their intimacy" (Ang 2022).

All of this is disrupted by the enervating entrance of a rowdy group of Maurice's friends, exclaiming they want tea after their successful cricket match (they talk of "wickets"). The men swiftly decouple when they hear the group barging in, Clive springing up to stand by the fireplace in mock nonchalance as Maurice stays seated. I am going to hazard a guess that Maurice stays seated because he is sexually aroused, which he does not want to reveal to the revellers and, perhaps, to Clive. Clive makes a silent exit but lingers for a moment, pensively, on the stairs.[6]

Maurice and his mates, in the next scene, head out to find refreshments, and suddenly Clive, lurking in a shadowy alley, appears and takes Maurice aside. "I know you read those books in the vac," Clive says, with a furtive excitement, referring to *The Symposium* and the like. "You'll understand, I don't have to explain." Clive provides the uncomprehending Maurice an explanation: "That I love you." Maurice's response expresses shock: "Don't talk rubbish." Steely yet stricken, Clive simply stares at his friend, then dashes away. Maurice confusedly calls out to him before rejoining the rowdy gang.

To use modern parlance, Maurice is not out to himself. The following three scenes chart this coming out process. In the grand dining hall where all stand formally dressed, Clive gives a speech in Latin as he, diffidently, and Maurice, gravely, stare at one another across the tables. (Ivory gives us a subtle sense

Figure 21
Maurice explains that he loves Clive, "in your very own way."

that Cornwallis carefully monitors this exchange of looks.) Clive returns to his rooms and finds Maurice waiting for him there, pleading for understanding. When Maurice approaches Clive, the latter snaps at his earnest friend, saying, "No – *don't* reopen it," in an emphatic manner that Hugh Grant specializes in, signalling that Clive is dangerous in anger. Maurice fumbles, "I thought it was the worst crime on the calendar." He adds, however, that he does love Clive, "in your very own way." When Clive expresses qualified gratitude that at least Maurice did not report him to the authorities, Maurice spits out, "Damn you, Durham," and exits.

A humorous and ardent nighttime scene follows, a witty parody of typical illicit-romance scenes in heterosexual love plots that anticipates Alec's sexual rescue of Maurice. Clive lies in bed asleep as Maurice climbs up to a window and comes inside. He goes to Clive, now awakened, and Clive, surprised but clearly touched and pleased, quietly says, "I love you," and Maurice responds, "I love you," and both men kiss. No sooner has this sealed declaration occurred than Maurice is back out the window, reversing his recent action.

I remember, when seeing this film in New York City in its initial release, how funny the audience found this scene, which plays like absurdist comedy. Notable as well is the lush appearance of the slumbering Clive, in a sumptuous night coat. He looks like a fantasy of a sensual young Oscar Wilde, adding to the heightened ambiance.

Perhaps the most purely exhilarating moment in the film comes next. Happily connected, giddily so, Maurice and Clive embark, wearing borrowed goggles, on a day trip to the countryside in a motor bicycle–cum–sidecar, leaving Cambridge and disapproving Dean Cornwallis behind. Sitting in the sidecar, Clive delightfully remarks, "Look out – it's the dean!" Maurice roars them past the harumphing dean, who commands, "Stop when I am talking to you!" This scene further establishes a pattern of Clive seducing Maurice into authority-defying trouble.

This is a momentous occasion, the scene where Maurice and Clive will finally be properly intimate, and the director, adapters, composer, cinematographer, and actors all rise to the challenge. The scene of the men with their bodies coiled as they lie in the grass begins with a shot of hands, linking this scene to the one where they first made physical contact. Grasping Clive's outstretched hand, Maurice squeezes, encompasses it. Then he tumbles onto Clive's body, lying supine on the earth. Ivory gives us a closeup of these hands, Maurice's fingers entering the empty spaces between Clive's fingers, but the closeup does not itself reveal the identity of the men, who become their merging hands.

It is only through repeat viewings that we can see that the hand that did the grasping and encompassed the other is Maurice's. So, when Maurice grasps Clive's hand, Clive allows this grasp to linger and then uses this shared clasp to throw Maurice on the ground beside him.

Figure 22
An indelible image of desire's kindling and renunciation at once.

Ivory's precise physical blocking of the actors always conveys thematic meaning. The hands (one cannot help recalling the significance of these extremities to the love declarations of Romeo and Juliet) metonymize the lovers, suggesting that Maurice is the dominant partner in that he takes hold of the hand raised, ready and waiting, in the air. And Maurice does take the lead in initiating physical intimacy when both lie on the ground. But Clive's passivity exerts its own dominance as he uses his hand to overthrow Maurice.

On the ground, Clive talks of "going through life half-awake" had Maurice had "the decency to leave me alone," to which the hero responds, "Perhaps we woke up each other." All the while, Maurice rubs Clive's chest and kisses him, his desire palpable. Maurice takes Clive's face in his hands and verges on bringing their lips together, but Clive protests, moving his mouth away from the man atop him, insisting, "No." "Can't you kiss me?" Maurice asks, passionately and frustratedly. Clive explains, "I think it would bring us down," squelching

Maurice's and the audience's hopes. Clive explains that they share a oneness and intimacy no woman could ever guess at, though clearly one that cannot in his view extend to the sexual.

◆ ◆ ◆

As is now well-known from Forster's papers, including his "sex diary," fore-grounded in Wendy Moffat's biography of Forster as a homosexual visionary, the author knew all about sexual frustration and inexperience when he wrote *Maurice*. Travels to India and Egypt during the First World War – his Red Cross service allowing him to escape military combat – facilitated a sexual breakthrough of the kind Mediterranean travels have famously given gay men for centuries.

Forster had begun to view his celibacy as "moral cowardice" and deter-mined to change his sexual status. He finally had sex in 1917 when he was thirty-eight, with a wounded soldier in Alexandria. "On the beach at Mon-tazah … suspended between terror and courage, he found a recuperating sol-dier as hungry as himself. The sex was brief and anonymous," the latter quality troubling the author despite his personal exposure to the homosexual Greek poet Cavafy's celebration of such trysts (Moffatt 2010, 147–8).

Forster did go on to experience an intensely intimate and sexual relation-ship with an Arab Egyptian, Mohammed El Adl, a consumptive who sadly died at twenty-three. (David Santos Donaldson's 2022 novel *Greenland* fea-tures a protagonist writing a novel from the perspective of El Adl.) Eventually, Forster would meet a married policeman, Bob Buckingham, who became his lover of many years (and Bob's wife a close friend, both being present at the writer's deathbed). Forster made Maurice everything he was not: hale, phys-ically beautiful, intellectually bereft, callow. But in one regard, the ability to love and the experience of having that love's sexual fulfillment denied, he gave Maurice his own heart.

James Wilby's performance contains marvellous subtle depths. "Can't you kiss me?" Maurice asks Clive, and the line reading conveys both physical and emotional deprivation and hunger. He and Hugh Grant, so well-cast, offer a powerful visual realization of a late-Victorian/Edwardian fantasy of homosexual desire. Each distinctly and equally beautiful, blond Maurice contrasted with brunet Clive, and in beautiful period clothing (Richard Dyer has emphasized the queer resonances of the sartorial), the actors embody many people's images of a halcyon homosexual past. If our twenty-first-century eyes interrogate this image as one propped up by the privileges of whiteness, which extends to the entire question of heritage cinema as a "white cinema," it must also be acknowledged that this is an exquisitely well-realized adaptation of Forster's writing that stands on its own as an aesthetic vision. I can think of few scenes of sexual passion enflamed and then renounced that have more finesse and power onscreen.

Maurice is sent down by an irate Dean Cornwallis, who tells him to take the noon train and that he will not be readmitted unless he writes the dean a letter of apology. In perhaps the first sign of his deepening political consciousness as a gay man, Maurice, boarding the train as Clive sees him off, remarks to his friend that had it been a "girl in that sidecar," the dean would have never so disciplined him ("Everybody cuts lectures."). When asked what he'll do, Maurice explains that he will get a job in the stock market, just like his father. (In the novel, Maurice does eventually relent and write a letter of apology to the dean and return to school, but the film makes no indication that Maurice does any of these things.)

This train departure scene, though emotionally muted, cites the Hollywood melodrama – distraught but heroically contained Bette Davis saying goodbye to train-bound Paul Henreid in *Now, Voyager* (Irving Rapper, 1942) – that the film will eventually evoke, as we will discuss in the last chapter. And one cannot help but think of the devastating train station farewell and last scene between Elio and Oliver in the Ivory-scripted *Call Me by Your Name*.

Figure 23
Maurice says goodbye to Clive (temporarily) and university (permanently).

At home, Dr Barry stealthily chastises Maurice for not being a "gentleman" enough to apologize to the dean and for bullying his mother. The kind, dim Mrs Hall listens outside the door along with Kitty as Dr Barry makes his criticisms plain. Maurice adamantly insists that he will not apologize to the dean, to his mother's chagrin and sparking Kitty's contempt. This scene indicates that Maurice remains immature and does not treat the women in his life respectfully. "Both were misogynists, Clive especially," Forster's narrator says of the men (100), and the film concurs.

Maurice finally visits Clive at his family estate, Pendersleigh (changed from Penge in the novel – the new name must have sounded more posh for American ears). The screenplay deftly expands on the novel's class discourse, Maurice's fish-out-of-water social anxieties. Maurice has travelled by carriage along

Figure 24
Violating class protocols at Pendersleigh, Maurice reaches out to shake Mrs
Durham's hand.

with a friend of Mrs Durham's. When this friend, Mrs Sheepshanks, emerges
from the carriage, she and the immediately formidable Mrs Durham (Judy
Parfitt) embrace, Clive's mother addressing her friend as "Woolly dear." (Maria
Britneva, also known as Maria St Just, plays Mrs Sheepshanks. The Russian
Britneva was a good friend of Tennessee Williams and his literary executor.
Her home was used as the setting for Pendersleigh.) But when Mrs Durham
and Maurice meet, he puts his hand out for her to shake, and she, just barely,
extends her own. Clearly, Maurice has misread the codes, taking the familiarity
just displayed between Mrs Durham and her friend as precedent and violating
protocol with his handshake. Looser about class stigma, Clive wryly informs
Maurice, when he mentions having no riding clothes, "Well, I can't associate
with you in that case."

Figure 25
Surreptitious (if celibate) same-sex pleasures: Maurice reacts with alarm, Clive
with indifference, to the appearance of Milly the maid.

Further class lessons await our hero. Tucked away in a remote room (Mrs
Durham signals that Maurice has been oddly banished), Maurice is suddenly
overtaken by a mischievous Clive, who, French farce-style, emerges from a
previously unseen door and hugs Maurice to the bed. Clive purposefully chose
this room to keep their intimacy more private and reduce Maurice's mandatory familial social interactions. As in the novel, the young men cuddle as
Milly, a shy, nervous housemaid porting a pitcher of water, enters, never looking at the supine males. Clive feels no anxiety whatsoever in the face of his
female servant, whereas Maurice appears to be bracing himself for trouble.
Class functions here as affect, the social differences between Clive and Maurice
indicated by the former's ease and indifference, the latter's guarded, error-
prone reserve.

Figure 26
Tender passions interrupted and surveilled: Maurice and Clive seen by Simcox at the Goblin House.

Maurice and Clive go riding the next morning (sticking to their plan in opposition to plans made by Clive's mother and sister, Pippa [Catherine Rabett]), stopping off at a small building that Clive identifies as "The Goblin House," built by his grandfather's grandfather. In the steamy, forested morning air, Clive and Maurice embrace by the door of the building. Maurice's tan sweater offsets his tousled blond locks, and Clive's gray sweater does the same for his brunet ones. The covert atmosphere and the men's contrasted beauty lend themselves to an overall erotic tone, complemented by their embrace. It is the most sexually charged scene between them in the film. But it is disrupted by the sudden appearance of Simcox (Patrick Godfrey), the Durhams' chief servant, bicycling. Simcox, whom Godfrey endows with a creepy, knowing, carefully contained smugness, pointedly and somewhat fearlessly stares down the embracing men, whose intimacy dissipates and ends.

The image of the men embracing outside of the Goblin House has become iconic. It represents Ivory's vision much more than it adheres to the source material. In the novel, this scene makes no mention of the patriarchal Durham Goblin House, nor does it depict the men being intimate; and there is no mention of Simcox or any other interruption. Instead, Forster writes, simply, near the end of chapter 17, "they were riding through the glades alone" (96).

The heritage film frequently makes the house a central figure – as *Howards End* exemplifies. Here, the Goblin House in its relatively small stature and clandestine, almost ethereal setting both metonymizes the houses of heritage cinema and parodies the metaphor, but it also begins to suggest something of a queer alternate space, a kind of "goblin" version of establishment settings and sexualities. The boathouse of Alec's fevered imaginings of secret sex with Maurice, eventually the site of their climactic, affirming reunion, emerges as a more substantive such space.

Some time passes; it is now 1911. A montage of sorts updates us about the men's post-university lives. Now mustachioed, the bourgeois Maurice has joined his late father's stockbroking firm, Hill & Hall, a private business based in the financial City of London; Clive studies for the bar; and they both socialize in tuxedos at Clive's fashionable London house.

In an interesting touch, voiceovers from Mrs Hall and Mrs Durham, taken from their correspondence where they compare notes about their sons' activities, frame the montage. Set to Richard Robbins's characteristically wistful and lyrical score, the voiceovers have a simultaneously gentle and tense quality. Though they never interact onscreen, the women maintain an epistolary intimacy. The fatherless sons live in families presided over by their mothers. These women could not be more distinct yet crucially share the defining circumstance that their sons are in love with one another.

Subtly, the matching voiceovers simultaneously convey the women's obliviousness to this fact and the intimacy it facilitates between them. Matchmaking Mrs Durham, concerned over whether Clive has a woman in his life (which she grilled Maurice about at a Pendersleigh dinner: "*Is* there someone, Mr

Figure 27
Risley appeals to Clive for help. Jhabvala's contribution was to turn Risley's homosexual scandal into the catalyst for Clive's straight turn.

Hall? Some Newnham girl?"), aims to invite Ada for the purpose of marrying
off her son (even if his marriage will mean Mrs Durham's eviction from the
main estate, which Clive has inherited, and transition to the dower house).

Pointedly, Mrs Durham's voiceover is punctuated by the sudden appearance
of Alec Scudder (Rupert Graves), the Durhams' young, roguish-looking gamekeeper. Mrs Durham cannot recall his name as she asks him to post her letter
to Mrs Hall. "Scudder, ma'am," Alec replies, in a tone through which Graves,
emphasizing the hard consonants in "Scudder," marvellously conveys a subtle
scorn at this rich woman who fails even to recall his name. (He will humor-
ously complain of this in bed with Maurice.)

Risley, persuasively played by Mark Tandy, reaches out to Clive for support
and legal advice, but he decisively rejects these requests. Guilty and furtive,

clumsily trying to hide his face from the defendant, Clive goes to Risley's sentencing. Before passing sentence, the judge harshly condemns Risley, emphasizing that he has used his elevated class position to corrupt his social inferior and that his promising political career is over. After the sentencing, Risley spots Clive in the crowd and gives him a long, accusatory stare. The strong implication is that the two men have been since their university days very much aware of each other as fellow homosexuals and that Risley feels contempt for the man who refuses to stand by his side now.

The film adheres to Forster's narrative by featuring Clive, alone, brooding away in sunlit Greece, silently mulling over things. When he returns home from Greece, he will break things off between them, devastating Maurice. But even before Clive visits the Mediterranean, trouble clearly brews between them. Clive broods in London too, keeping a chilly distance from Maurice, at times almost a roommate. At a concert hall, Clive arrives late, and Clive, irritated by Maurice's concern, snaps, "I don't want to be nannied." At Clive's London home, a young woman asks if Maurice's mustache "will be the making of him," and Clive retorts, "I think it's revolting." After the guests have left, Maurice and Clive prepare for bed, Maurice removing Clive's cufflinks, Clive perfunctorily loosening Maurice's bowtie before pointedly going into his own room and closing the door shut on Maurice. It's as if we were watching a gay *Scenes from a Marriage*, the long-term couple rotely attending to one another and passionlessly separate. All these moments prepare us to expect Clive's thoroughly closed-off attitude once he returns from Greece.

Before leaving for Greece and after Risley's sentencing, a shaken Clive, who has passed the bar exam, attends a candlelit celebratory dinner at the Halls'. Surrounded by Maurice and his family, all toasting him, Clive becomes wretchedly ill and falls out of his seat to the floor, yanking the tablecloth and dishes with him. Some comedic moments follow when Maurice, having told his sisters to get help and supplies, instructs his befuddled mother to aid Clive: "Fan." "What?" "Fan, *fan* him." She dutifully, feebly complies. Once

Clive revives, Maurice kisses him on the lips, resulting in his mother's even more befuddled "Oh!" Later, when they have put Clive to bed, Maurice instructs his mother not to mention that he kissed Clive. "We're great friends, relations almost," Maurice explains to his kind-hearted mother, who smiles understandingly and clasps him reassuringly on the shoulder. Clive, however, wants none of Maurice's ministrations. Frustrated at being chucked out of Clive's sickroom to make way for the arrival of a nurse, Maurice huffily complains. The house-call-making physician wryly retorts, "We'll have you wheeling the baby next."

Clive alarms Maurice the next day by making an abrupt exit, accompanied by his mother (who remains uncharacteristically wordless). Maurice rushes home and climbs into the carriage next to Clive. In a furtive and tender gesture, Maurice puts his coat over the men's arms so that he can secretly clasp Clive's hand. But Clive will have none of this former intimacy's return and unclasps. He also calls out for his mother to join him so that he can escape.

As if emerging from a chrysalis, the anxiously prostrate Clive returns to his former vigour with a key difference: he will now determinedly present himself as straight, encouraging Maurice to do the same. At a formal dinner that the Halls attend at a posh London venue, Clive suddenly makes a toast. "Maurice, come," he instructs, raising his glass and addressing the women: "The *ladies*." Although he had done the student film *Privileged* and some television work, Grant was making his big-screen debut in *Maurice*, and his deft handling of the opaque, even inscrutable Clive always impresses. "Grant has a nifty profile," Pauline Kael remarked, praising his performance. "It suggests a sexy-aesthete rotter. He's amusingly untrustworthy" (Kael 1989, 361). Here, Grant imbues Clive's toast with a lacerating cheerfulness, simultaneously conveying a rebuke of Maurice and a willed merriment.

Clive travels to Greece despite his mother's protest, which she conveys to Maurice along with her hopes that her son will go to America instead. "He must see America and, if possible, the colonies," she explains. "But not Greece,

Mr Hall. That is travelling for pleasure." Maurice adds that he would prefer going to America himself. Is it possible that Mrs Durham speaks from a place of anxiety about her son's sexual leanings, which would apparently be inflamed by the seductions of the Mediterranean?

Clive walks through lovely sunlit vistas, a solitary, somewhat glum figure juxtaposed against classical ruins. He sits and reads one of the many letters Maurice has sent him and to which Clive will not respond. In the novel, Clive sits in "the theatre of Dionysius" (116) located in Athens. The film swaps in the Greek theatre at Segesta, near Castellammare in northwest Sicily.

Maurice's epistolary voiceover plays over images of Clive sitting in the Mediterranean sunlight, surrounded by ancient architecture. Merchant Ivory excels at such moments of introspection and wistful, brooding solitude, always conveyed through the beauty of the images in contrast to the plangency of the Richard Robbins score. The atmosphere is lyrical yet tense, Robbins's score enhancing, enlarging, and clarifying the action and its emotional stakes.

Maurice chides Clive for not writing, yearningly asking him to do so. Clive's correspondent fills up his letter with reports of his life ("Still no word from you, so here is my news"). He explains that "in the darkest reaches of Bermondsey" (in South East London, now quite a fashionable up-and-coming area) he teaches "the dockers lads at the mission" "the gentle art of boxing." A montage accompanies these words and shows Maurice in the ring. The fusion of voiceover, montage, and lyrical music is a distinctive Merchant Ivory touch.

Maurice self-deprecatingly notes that, ostensibly the boxing expert, it is he who receives the "pummeling" although it pales in comparison to the one that Clive gave him at the Wigmore Hall. "Ha ha," adds the letter-writer, a softening comic tone. Maurice's reference to the brief Wigmore Hall scene, where Clive arrived late and responded testily to Maurice's "nannying," indicates, despite attempts to make light of it, Maurice's enduring hurt over this moment, which he, rightly, took as a warning sign. Maurice next expresses concerns about Clive's health. All the while, Clive, reading the letter, remains removed, stonily silent. The disconnection runs deep.

Without letting Maurice know his arrival date, Clive returns to England and stops off at the Halls'. Kitty and Ada, taking "an ambulance course," make Clive their prop, wrapping him in bandages, simulating wounds, taking his temperature. Hugh Grant's marvellous deadpan conveys Clive's comic protests ("Ow! That really hurt!"). Speaking with Ada as she mummifies him, Clive marvels at her speech. "You sound just like Maurice. Your voices are wonderfully alike."

Mrs Durham has been trying to set up Clive and Ada, and Clive does appear to respond to her favourably. If he does feel heterosexual desire, naturally he would be attracted to the lovely and appealing Ada. That Clive marvels at her Maurice-like voice (Mrs Hall adds that she also has his nose and mouth, while Kitty has his brains) suggests that he is attempting to discover a female substitute for his once-loved friend.

In many fictions, homosexual desire and/or a relationship function as preparation for an inevitable heterosexual outcome. Forster's contemporary Evelyn Waugh foregrounds this sexual narrative in his famous novel *Brideshead Revisited* (1945), whose protagonist Charles Ryder falls in love with a fellow university student, the aristocratic Lord Sebastian Flyte. His love for Sebastian prefigures his mature love for Sebastian's sister Julia. In keeping with this pattern, Clive wills himself into sexual normalcy by discovering the appeal of Maurice replicated in his sister's qualities.

When Maurice, cleanshaven in the letter-reading montage but once again mustachioed (Clive was right about its disfiguring effect) and barely able to contain his excitement over Clive's return, at last comes home, he discovers the bandaged Clive and immediately begins unravelling him ("Oh, Clive, why did you let them"). Having done so, Maurice beams at his unfettered friend, clasping his shoulders from the front: "I say he looks *well*." Maurice wastes no time jettisoning female company ("No, girls, not you") and getting Clive alone in a separate study.

Maurice embraces Clive, who stiffly raises unembracing arms and rejects the offer of a drink. Maurice gently and tensely teases Clive for not having written him. Clive flatly remarks, "Maurice, I don't want a row," which leads his friend to respond, "*I* do. I want a row, and I'll have it!" Maurice pours Clive's drink into his own. Wilby adds a disarming antic quality to Maurice's awkward attempts at flirtation and banter, especially since he must negotiate his disappointment with his friend and joy at their reunion.

Clive proceeds to explain to Maurice that they must alter the previous terms of their relationship. He has thought about it deeply and has decided that "We've got to change, you and I." To which Maurice, ruffling Clive's floppy locks, responds, "Can the leopard change his spots?" As this exchange grows increasingly intense, Ivory's camera, while it fluidly negotiates the limited space of the study, keeps the men tightly enclosed within it. The spatial strictures poignantly match the emotional ones.

As we have discussed, the film "corrects" Clive's conversion to heterosexuality by motivating it much more explicitly as a reaction to Risley's trial and imprisonment. *The Advocate*'s Marcia Pally, in her 1987 article on the making of the film, describes Clive's declaration to Maurice here as pointedly distinct from the novel's version. "Ivory and Hesketh-Harvey ... changed Clive's confession to Maurice. In the book, his newfound heterosexuality is all a muddle and a mystery to Clive. 'I have become normal – like other men,' Clive tells Maurice in despair ... 'I've changed, I've changed.' In the film, Clive says, 'We must change [you and I].' The effect is much more political, much more a desperate response to prejudice – especially following Risley's tragedy." As Ivory explained to Pally, he did not "intend the script to be more political." He observes that while Clive is indeed affected by "the law and prejudice," his sexual conversion reflects the emergence of his "basic orthodoxy," and the screenwriters' changes in his lines "just made it emerge faster and more dramatically, more cinematically" (Pally 1987, 109).

As the remarkably compressed and increasingly violent scene unspools in the film, Maurice maintains that Clive, "in a muddle," has forgotten that he and Maurice are "outlaws" and can only trust one another. "I risk everything, and gladly," Maurice explains to Clive, "because the one thing I dread losing is you." Maurice's penchant for rebellion, his willingness to embrace outlaw status, belies his priggish sensibility and foretells his daring relationship with Alec. Far from persuading Clive, Maurice's risk-taking stance only increases his friend's intractability. He encourages Maurice to consider how wonderful marriage with a woman would be. After listing all that normality can give them if they just embrace it, Clive, in response to Maurice's declaration that the two men love one another, snaps, "If I were in love with anyone now, then it would be with some nice girl. Like Ada." Maurice, dumbstruck, says, "Ada?"

Maurice, suspecting a romantic plot brewing between his sister and Clive, calls for Ada. "You can't drag in a woman. I won't have it," Clive protests, barring Maurice from opening the door. Their struggle leads Maurice desperately to kiss him. And bite him: he draws blood. Clive pushes Maurice off; he lands in a chair and begins to weep as Clive daubs his bloody lip. Maurice sobs messily and pitiably, lamenting, "What an ending! What an ending!" The men's scuffle has attracted Ada's attention, and Clive goes out to talk with her. Maurice bolts the door behind him, weeping and shaking as Clive asks him to unlock the door ("Maurice, don't be an ass"). Maurice sounds desperate notes: "What's gonna happen to me? I'm done for." Wilby's acting is harrowing here: Maurice feebly, desperately embraces himself as he sputters, a gesture at once defensive and abject.

The lowest point of Maurice's life is yet to come. After Clive has left, Maurice sits by the evening fire, and Ada cautiously approaches him. Maurice unleashes his rage, deprivation, betrayal, and self-loathing on Ada. He cruelly lies to her, saying that Clive accused her of throwing herself at him, trying to "corrupt him," spitefully adding that she has "the satisfaction" of knowing that she has destroyed their friendship. Ada, weeping herself, simply responds, "You've always been unkind to us. Always." Maurice responds: "It's not my fault."

Maurice seems acutely aware that Ada – without his passionate intensity – could have access to Clive bodily as well as emotionally and maritally, all the forms of possession denied her brother. Nothing excuses Maurice's wretched treatment of her, but this is a point worth making. Ada approaches her clearly troubled brother, who sits staring into the fireplace after Clive departs.[7] In an exquisite depiction of the closet and its stifling of direct speech or contact, Ada can find no language to comfort Maurice or inquire about why he is so distraught. Maurice, obtuse as ever, fails to recognize her sympathy and care and miserably taunts her. Does Ada have some sense that he loves Clive? She cannot put it into words, can only say, in response to Maurice's cutting questions, "Nothing."

In a subtle sign of growth, Maurice shaves off the disfiguring "manly" mustache and returns to his clean-shaven beauty. We see him again, in the ring and teaching boxing. Inside the locker room, surrounded by men changing out of their athletic garb, Maurice sits on a bench, for a time a clothed body in a sea of cheerfully naked men. He pulls off his shirt and gazes at frolicking, muscled lads roughhousing in the showers, splashing each other, laughing. (One thinks of the beautiful section 11 of "Song of Myself" in Whitman's 1855 *Leaves of Grass*, which begins, "Twenty-eight young men bathe by the shore, / Twenty-eight young men and all so friendly / Twenty-eight years of womanly life and all so lonesome.") Ivory's painterly eye indelibly captures these lithe male forms animated by the young men's infectious mirth. He also captures, as does Wilby, the deprivation in Maurice's haunted eyes as he stares at these alluring and unreachable bodies.

Maurice's mother receives a letter from Mrs Durham one morning. "Children," Mrs Hall addresses her offspring as she reports the news. Clive is to marry "the Lady Anne Woods." Interestingly, Mrs Hall makes no particular address to Maurice, simply announces the news to all present. Kitty reads the letter herself and tells her daffy mother that she has gotten it wrong, saying Clive is marrying "the lady, Anne Woods."

Mrs Hall and Kitty leave the room. Ada and Maurice are seated the breakfast table when she quietly asks him, "Do you know her, Maurice?" He quietly responds, "Oh, yes." Apparently, Clive met her in Greece.

Maurice's redemption begins here. He addresses Ada before she too leaves: "Ada, I behaved badly to you after Clive's last visit. He never said those things

I let you think he said. He never blamed you." Ada, for her part, as Helena Michell subtly plays her, responds very simply, "I don't care whether he did. It doesn't signify. I love Arthur now." She refers to Maurice's university chum Chapman. Maurice presses on, gentle of voice and affectingly sincere: "Chapman's a good fellow. For two people in love, to marry strikes me as very jolly. I wish you happiness." That Maurice can feel remorse about how he treated Ada and that he can, finally, think of someone else indicates his maturation and newfound empathy, shifts beautifully conveyed by Wilby's cautious, sincere delivery. The movie softens the novel's version of this scene, where Ada does not resist the temptation to dig into Maurice's feelings of loss and responds to his congratulations with passive-aggressive circumlocutions. I prefer the film's version, which allows us to see Maurice's growth and, without sentimentalizing her, does not portray Ada as vindictive, just self-protectively contained.

Clive finally contacts Maurice himself about the impending nuptials, putting Anne on the phone. Phoebe Nicholls, playing Anne, is sweetly charming in this scene, saying in a musical voice that Maurice is the eighth friend of Clive's she's spoken to that day. ("The *eighth*?" Maurice retorts.) This is without question Anne's most appealing moment in the film. The men make plans for Maurice to visit. In a brief scene, we see Clive and Anne marry, and Maurice, alone as always, looking at them in a crowd from afar. (A subtle touch: we see the shadowy presence of Scudder behind him in the wedding crowd and the odious servant Simcox, glowering at Maurice.)

In the most unpleasant moment of the film, Maurice brutally retaliates against an older man who comes on to him in a train car compartment. (Alan Foss plays the character listed in the credits as "Old Man on Train.") Wilby uses an ugly angry expression to convey Maurice's self-disgust as well as his disgust with the man.

Distraught, Maurice futilely consults Dr Barry to discover why he's sexually aberrant. The doctor inspects his genitals and pronounces them "clean," thinking an STD is his patient's crisis. When he learns the real nature of the problem

– Maurice self-loathingly lumps himself in with Risley and Oscar Wilde – Dr Barry instructs Maurice never to discuss it again: "No, sir, I'll not discuss! The worst thing I could do for you is to discuss." That this scene is performed by a gay/bisexual actor, Denholm Elliott, playing a homophobic doctor, and a straight actor, Wilby, playing an agonized gay man, adds a layer of metatextual queer irony to the proceedings.[8] Indeed, the casting of another gay actor, Simon Callow, in the role of the headmaster who instructs young Maurice in the mysteries of heterosexual intercourse and marriage has already signalled this queer knowingness.

Maurice visits Pendersleigh in autumn 1913, arriving when Clive, embarking on a political career, is out canvassing. Maurice and Archie (Michael Jenn), Clive's sister Pippa's cheerful and dull husband, walk the verdant grounds in the morning and shoot rabbits, which are then bagged up by the gamekeeper Alec Scudder, who walks behind the men. (Maurice does not shoot.)

The movie characteristically takes its time to establish the improbable circumstances of Maurice and Alec's romance. Maurice demonstrates little interest in Alec at first, always treating him, as does Archie, desultorily as a servant. When Alec inquires if the men want to head back due to the increasing mist, Archie speaks of him as if he were not present: "I suppose he thinks it's *our* fault."

The cheeky Alec finds ways to make his presence felt, however. Maurice wistfully mentions to Archie that today happens to be his birthday. Back in the changing room where the men take off their boots and after Archie has left, Alec wishes Maurice a happy birthday, and he gives the gamekeeper a blank look that signals little interest in his unusual gesture. Alec goes out of his way to express hopes that Maurice will return to Pendersleigh soon. When Maurice, perhaps worn down by the gamekeeper's chattiness, asks him about his impending trip to the Argentine, Alec remarks, "Have you ever been there yourself, sir?" Given Alec's brash contempt for the likes of Mrs Durham, who does not remember his name when she asks him to post a letter, his consistent respect for Maurice establishes that he can, like Maurice, break the ranks of

Figure 28
Alec asks Maurice, in reference to Alec's planned emigration to Argentina,
"Have you ever been there yourself, sir?"

class to align with his beloved. When snide Simcox makes derisive noises
about Maurice, Alec immediately counters, "Mr Hall is a *gentleman*," and
Simcox snorts.

Some scenes gain renewed interest when we know that Maurice and Alec
will eventually "unite," as the hypnotist Mr Lasker Jones puts it. No scene occurs in this film without a past or future meaning embedded within it. For
example, what seems like a throwaway scene begins almost invisibly to blur
the lines between middle-class Maurice and Alec, "one of the roughs," to wax
Whitmanian. The Durhams and guests have after-dinner libations in the
piano room when a leak in the ceiling demands that the piano be moved.
Clive calls it a night for the Durhams, leaving the logistics of leaks and piano-
moving to the servants. But Maurice quietly assists Alec in moving the piano

after all the others have retired (Simcox joins in, but only after we get a clear shot of Maurice and Scudder together moving the piano). Incidentally, this scene also contains the pithiest depiction, perhaps, of the Durhams' attitude toward servants. When the young maid Milly (the one who brought in the pitcher of water to Maurice's room) appears in the room to help with the leakage, Mrs Durham informs her witheringly, "We had to ring twice. *Twice.*" As Mrs Durham, Judy Parfitt deploys her naturally stern, sharp features to good classist effect here.

All the while, Alec insinuates himself into Maurice's company, telling him, as they stand by that fateful, stairway-to-heaven ladder, that it's good to see Maurice back at Pendersleigh, causing Maurice to look at him askance. Alec spies on Maurice in the evenings. Reversing the typical trajectory of homosexual procuring in such narratives, it is the working-class male who gazes with desire at the upper-class male and fantasizes about possessing him.

Before the famous nighttime seduction scene when Alec climbs into Maurice's bedroom and initiates their sexual encounter, the gamekeeper voyeuristically watches Maurice during a previous evening's rainstorm. From a low-level POV long shot, we watch – along with Alec, as if we were him – Maurice emerge from his room high above, stick his blond locks out of his window, douse his head with the rain, and utter his own kind of barbaric yawp. All of this excites and charms Alec, who approvingly guffaws.

This scene works meaningfully on several levels. It establishes Alec's libidinous and emotional fascination and identification with Maurice and reminds us of Maurice's capacity for transgression. Part of what delights Alec so much is seeing this upper-class gentleman literally and vigorously letting his hair down. He taps into the transgressive potential that makes Maurice – like himself – a daring person.

All this time, Maurice has begun seeking the conversion therapy services of the American hypnotist Mr Lasker Jones, played, in an inspired casting, by Ben Kingsley. Kingsley's stylized American accent and demeanour lend the part an aptly uncanny and quite funny quality. Maurice lies on a table as Lasker

Figure 29
Alec climbing down the fateful ladder to chat up Maurice.

Jones hypnotizes him, making him see a portrait on a wall and a widening crack in the carpet that he jumps over.

The hypnotist encourages Maurice to appreciate the inviting prettiness of the portrait's subject, "Miss Edna May." Maurice plaintively responds, "I want to go home to my mother," and then oddly laughs, perhaps at how vulnerable his response makes him sound. Encouraging him to respond favourably to her long pretty hair, Maurice stammers, "I like short hair best," and when asked why begins inarticulately to cry. In the next scene, Lasker Jones favourably observes that Maurice is open to suggestion and that he was able to see the images put into his mind. In a moment that made the audience laugh when I saw the film the year it was released, Lasker Jones advocates manly exercises to the departing Maurice: "A little tennis. Stroll around with a gun."

As we discussed in the chapter on the novel, the hypnotist stands in for Freudian psychoanalysis and the benefits of the talking cure. (This is not to say that Freud would ever have endorsed conversion therapy.) Lasker Jones,

Figure 30
The hypnotist, Lasker Jones, beginning conversion therapy.

though an ambiguous figure, provides a welcome alternative to the repressive, silencing Dr Barry.

Maurice's trips into town lead to speculation on Anne Durham's part that Maurice has some girl in London, a supposition most enthusiastically embraced by Clive. He visits Maurice in his room at night to celebrate the news. In so doing, he interrupts Maurice's act of letter-writing (and Wilby's voiceover), a statement of "his condition as he understands it" for Lasker Jones. Clive didn't answer Maurice's letters, and now his entrance interrupts Maurice's written attempts to reflect on his sexuality.

Maurice stays seated at his desk while Clive stands and walks about, a characteristically visualized depiction of their disconnection. Clive simply beams over his newfound (and illusory) belief that Maurice has followed his heterosexual example. "Aren't women *extraordinary*?" Clive asks. Partly because he is trying to become straight, partly because he is resigned, and partly, I conjecture, to return Clive's glib callousness with emotional detachment, Maurice plays along, giving his former friend permission to "tell Anne. Tell everybody."

About Clive's mustache: it desexualizes him, just as it brought out an ugliness in Maurice. Like Maurice's earlier one, Clive's moustache signifies his rejection of his former beauty and adoption of a synthetic sexual façade. My intention is neither to say something for nor against mustaches but rather to identify one of Ivory's character motifs.

Clive takes Maurice's hand and kisses it, saying, "I just wanted to show that ... I hadn't forgotten the past." This perfunctory gesture speaks volumes, perfectly encapsulating the sexless constrictions Clive imposed on the men's previous relationship and his insistence on a hypocritical Platonism: hypocritical because Clive conceals his sexual anxieties, perhaps even revulsion at the body, within this ostensibly elevated idealism. Not that his relations with Anne indicate anything but functional commitment. She spies on him while she lies in their bed at night, and immediately closes her eyes when she catches a tantalizing glimpse of his beautiful, exposed posterior, his sculpted legs and buttocks. If Anne, his wife, considers Clive's body a forbidden object, for whom is it available? When he climbs into bed, he bestows a most perfunctory kiss on her.

"Quits, and I'll go," Clive says to Maurice, now standing on the opposite side of him and extending his own hand. Maurice kisses it, another static gesture that he, unlike his former friend, understands as such. Increasingly insightful, Maurice no longer accepts Clive's sexual and emotional dictates even if he still humours them.

Unbeknownst to the men, their interactions stir someone else's imagination. From down below on the ground, Alec can see the men in the room and registers their homoerotic intimacy (such as it is). He will later use this information to get back at Maurice for rejecting and demeaning him.

Pauline Kael's pan of *Maurice*, one consistent with her usual response to Merchant Ivory films (*Room with a View* being the only one she – mildly –

praised), makes a point of *Maurice*'s belief that its hero gains clarity and humanity through his self-realization as gay. Kael faults both Forster and the film for presenting this idea so openly and sincerely, in a manner that echoes Cynthia Ozick's hostility towards the novel. Assigning Forster's novel to a "temporary madness" that also characterizes Norman Mailer and Katharine Hepburn in this three-pronged review, Kael complains that Maurice "isn't convincingly homosexual; he wouldn't be convincingly heterosexual, either. He isn't convincingly alive – he's a device that doesn't work." In her view, the misconceived character stymies Wilby, who can only give a decent performance once Maurice has had sex with Alec and learns what he wants. Kael's chief issue with the film and its source is the idea that "Maurice's full physical commitment to his homosexual drives is his redemption" (Kael 1989, 361). But what if it *is* his redemption? Gaining clarity about his sexuality sharpens Maurice's muddled mind, makes him more questioning of his seemingly inevitable fate of conformity and sexual nullity. Being able to see through Clive's armoured self-delusion is part of this clarity.

Maurice comes back, unexpectedly, to Pendersleigh the night before the nervously anticipated local cricket match involving servants and gentry. Clive and Anne are "electioneering overnight," so Maurice attends a grim dinner with Mrs Durham and Reverend Borenius (Peter Eyre), who obsesses over whether Alec will be confirmed when he settles in Argentina. (More class instruction from Mrs Durham: "Dinner jacket's enough tonight. I'm afraid we're only three." Though they look like tuxedos when worn with a bowtie, dinner jackets lack tails.)

Maurice enjoys a postprandial cigarette on the grounds. Alec emerges from the woods, a satyr of surprise, and intercepts him. The two men walk and talk briefly. For the first time, Maurice asks Alec a personal question, about his impending move to Argentina.

The men, walking alongside one another, could not be more distinct, handsome in ways entirely their own. The black dinner jacket Maurice wears gives him a distinguished air, especially as it contrasts with his uncovered, straight, Apollo-blond hair and the gold chain of his pocket watch. Alec, a Caravaggio Bacchus in workman's clothes, wears a soft gray woollen cap with hints of blue, a bulky gray overcoat with brown tones, a brown vest over a white shirt, an ensemble that brings out the dark earthiness of his curly hair and brown eyes. This moment of potential intimacy between them, the improbable but palpable frisson of their pairing, lays the groundwork for their imminent sexual intimacy.

The decision to make Maurice, dark-haired in the novel, a blond has sparked controversy. As Ivory explained to Robert Emmet Long, after Julian Sands left the project, he deliberated over which actor to cast in the lead, Wilby or Julian Wadham. "But as I'd already cast the dark-haired Hugh Grant as Clive, I decided on the blond James Wilby. When he reads this, he'll yell, 'What! The only reason Jim cast me was that I'm blond! Bloody hell!'" (Long 2005, 213). As noted, Wadham was cast in the small role of one of Maurice's fellow stockbrokers.

I think that Ivory's casting was brilliant, first because of Wilby's perfectly pitched performance, and second because the tall, blond Wilby so powerfully evokes Herman Melville's Billy Budd, the blond "Handsome Sailor." As I will have more opportunities to note, Melville's work is an intertext for Forster and Ivory both. A similar casting choice energizes Ang Lee's *Brokeback Mountain*, which savours the contrasts between Heath Ledger's taciturn blondness and Jake Gyllenhaal's brunet sensuality.

Maurice, filmed from a high angle, lies in bed at night, alone as always. His dreams make his sleep fitful. Full of images from the hypnotism session with Mr Lasker Jones, his dreams express his unconscious responses to the hypnotist's efforts. In a keen expression of heterosexual ambivalence, Maurice floats on a raft with a woman lying by his side, both fully clothed and grimly formal. They lie next to one another, but no bodily contact or intimacy exists. A superimposed image of Lasker Jones ceaselessly waving a metronome finger prods them fruitlessly on. Maurice dreams that he bails out the boat (linking him to Alec, who, Simcox reported at dinner, has bailed out the boat for the cricket match tomorrow). Robbins's score enhances the spooky quality of this oneiric portrait of a loveless union, Maurice's probable fate should he continue to follow the hypnotist's guidelines.

Waking up, Maurice, pajama-clad, walks to the window, opens it, and, oddly, rattles the ladder propped up against the roof near his window. (It has been used to "attack the roof" on Clive's instruction to repair the piano room leak.) Why does Maurice do this? His gesture indicates nervous energy and an attempt to shake it off, like his nighttime embrace of and submission to the rain.

In the Edwardian era of the closet's predominance, codes and signals that could be interpreted as invitations for sexual contact – in a word, cruising – were rife. In his excellent study *Queer London: Perils and Pleasures in the Sexual Metropolis, 1918–1957*, Matt Houlbrook describes, for example, the network of queer signals used by working-class youths looking for middle-class sexual marks (pickups known as "steamers") in the early twentieth century. "Invisible – for the most part – to passersby and policemen, they developed tactics that ensured they remained visible to each other. In the perpetual flux and movement of strangers, queer men could move unnoticed while making the streets bustling centers of queer life. Passing the crowd, they exchanged recognition signals of movement, gesture, and gaze," constructing and engaging in a "complex spatial poetics" of the streets (Houlbrook 2005, 46). This queer network of signals may account for why Alec believes Maurice, in shaking the ladder at night, is signalling to him that he wants sex. To be sure, Maurice seems to have no idea that he is doing this, which is not to say that he does not unconsciously *want* this.

"Was that you calling to me, sir?" Alec asks as he makes his way into Maurice's room via the ladder and the room's window, an echo of Maurice's ardent (though sex-free) climb into Clive's university room window. Most viewers of the film, to offer anecdotal evidence, understand Alec's decision to initiate sex with Maurice as motivated by secret knowledge of his proclivities; he just *knows* Maurice's nature. And this is supported by Alec's dialogue as he begins kissing Maurice and successfully rousing him: "It's all right. I know, sir." But it is also worth noting that Alec has interpreted Maurice's behaviour as code.

To describe the impact that this scene had in 1987 and the power it retains, I experienced it as a revelation akin to concrete evidence of the existence of extraterrestrial life. *Maurice* is a film about the closet and romantic rejection. It's also a film about sexual deprivation, an experience that Forster, who had not had sex until after he wrote *Maurice*, knew expertly. The nighttime setting, the gothic atmosphere of Maurice's room at night, his tousled sheets and restlessness, the image of Alec, illuminated by moonlight, surreptitiously making his way into the room through the window, the initially ominous notes in Robbins's score, Maurice's expression of bewilderment and panic as Alec approaches him (reminiscent of Poe's atmosphere of nighttime fear in his story "The Tell-Tale Heart"), the way that these motifs of fear cede to the ecstasy of submission, Maurice yielding to Alec's command ("Come on. Lie down."), the transition from ominous notes to rapture in Robbins's score: all these elements work together to simulate and convey Maurice's experience of sexual fulfillment at last. And Alec is so tender about it all.

A Melvillean atmosphere of sweetness and intimacy (*Moby-Dick*'s Ishmael and Queequeg on their "hearts' honeymoon" in bed together) sustains the men in their next scene. It is morning, and the men float on bodies pressed against each other in a sea of rumpled bedsheets. Alec, looking up at Maurice, says playfully (and pragmatically), "Sir, the church has struck. You'll have to release me." Atop him, Maurice instructs the gamekeeper to call him by his name: "*Maurice*. I'm Maurice."

Especially considering the time this film was made and released in, the homophobic atmosphere whipped into a frenzy during the height of the AIDS crisis, this scene is remarkable for showing naked men in bed together sharing

Figure 31
Maurice tells Scudder to call him by his first name, and Scudder verges on becoming "Alec." Maurice and Alec in the Russet Room during their glorious first postcoital morning.

a moment of intimacy between their living breathing fleshly bodies. Flesh against flesh, caresses, the stroking of tresses, all the somatic connections in the world that have so often been denied by the world, all so hard won.

Speaking about the day's impending cricket match and his chores including bailing out the boat, Alec remarks, "They told me that all young gentlemen learn to dive. Well, I never learned to. It seems more natural-like not to let your head get under the water. I call that drowning before your day." This dialogue has a touching unguardedness. Maurice responds that he was taught that illness would follow if he did not get his hair wet. Alec responds, perhaps playfully and almost provocatively, "Well, you was taught what wasn't the case." The screenplay hews to the lovely stylized language that Forster invents for Alec to convey his class differences from Maurice, including his euphemism for sex, "sharing." Here, Alec's comments about water and diving and drowning (one thinks of Junot Díaz's 1996 story "Drown," about a brief and perilous homosexual attachment between young men) lend his speech a fateful quality, something mournful and fragile.

Maurice, for his part, seems more openhearted and connected with Alec than he has with anyone else. He calls him Alec and asks him a very Forsterian question: "Did you ever dream you had a friend, someone to last your whole life?" For Maurice, perhaps for Alec as well, this sexual experience has been transformative and world-making, but on levels beyond sex and bodies, important as both are to the experience. What is moving and meaningful here is that the men connect on a personal level as well as a sexual and corporeal one, held together by "the divine magnet" that Herman Melville describes in one of his ardent letters to Nathaniel Hawthorne. (It's the kind of atmosphere that Andrew Haigh will create in his 2011 film *Weekend*.) When Maurice – and Wilby commits to the scene utterly – rests his head on Alec's chest as he asks him about surpassing friendship, he seems both relieved and spent, submitting to and wonderstruck by his wild luck.

The Park v. Village cricket match at Pendersleigh forces Maurice and Alec into a public interaction that occurs freshly after their surreptitious first lovemaking. Despite advice from Simcox that the servants want him to be the captain of their team ("Things always go better with a gentleman captain"), Maurice defers this honour, telling him to make Alec captain. The cricket match encapsulates a key element of Ivory's style, which is to let life happen, occur at its own pace, onscreen. While there are baroque, even expressionist passages in his films – Alec's nighttime seduction of Maurice, for example – a committed naturalism defines the better part of his aesthetic.

However languidly presented, the cricket match simmers with tensions along class and gay liberation lines that were important to Forster. This sequence is the clearest instance in Ivory's at times elliptical filmmaking where familiarity with Forster's novel is essential. While the match appears leisurely

Figure 32
Maurice joins the cricket match and, crucially, Alec, the two scoring against
the world.

and emblematic of Ivory's "slow cinema," and Ivory has discussed being bewildered, along with his American crew, by the national ritual of cricket, it
extends Forster's transgressive vision of same-sex desire as a battle against social oppression and the achievement of social equality in defiance of class
lines. If the cricket match appears "to be absurd and incomprehensible" and
indicates "the blinkering of interest and vision" on Forster's part, "the partnership at the wicket between Maurice and Alec comes to represent the
strength of their love and the promise of a redeemed and classless England."
Forster excels specifically at envisioning "a fusion of homosexuality and social
equality," which comes through in the graceful partnership of Maurice and
Alec during the match, one disrupted by the appearance of Clive, whose contribution to the game results in the end of this alliance (Singh 1996, 171).

As the cricket match unhurriedly proceeds, Ivory's cinema affords gay male and straight female viewers a great deal of pleasure, a visual feast of images of Maurice and Alec in their cricket uniforms. As some critics have noted, heritage cinema has long been a site for queer pleasure, the opportunity to see objects of desire in period clothing, the entire point of the cinema being to afford us the chance to contemplate the beauty of bodily presence onscreen, or so this cinema suggests.

In "Homosexuality and Heritage," Richard Dyer emphasizes the importance of the sartorial to the heritage film and depictions of same-sex desire and queer men. "Queer masculinity has characteristically been represented as something abnormal, informed by ideas of sickness (queers as emaciated, cadaverous, pale or just plain weird looking) and effeminacy (plucked eyebrows, prissy lips or exaggerated feminine fleshiness). In heritage cinema, on the other hand, queers were shown as indistinguishable from other nicely turned out, worth looking at men." He continues: "Good-looking clothes also facilitate the exploration of what men may find attractive in each other" (Dyer 2002, 218).

The cricket match dovetails with the nude male bathing scene in *A Room with a View*. Like that scene, where the characters played by Julian Sands, Rupert Graves, and Simon Callow skinny-dip and cavort in a pond, the cricket match offers a leisurely chance to contemplate the beauty of the male form. In a nod to that film, its singular star Helena Bonham-Carter makes a cameo appearance here as a cricket-match spectator who initially makes somewhat acid comments about Alec's cricket match captaincy to Pippa but later more appreciative ones about his physical appeal.

After Clive joins the match, Maurice sits behind Alec and a friend of his as they speak privately. It certainly seems like they are speaking about Maurice behind his back. At this, Maurice gets up and walks away, indicating his growing suspicions about Alec. For all we know, Alec has extolled the beauty of Mr Hall's naked form to his endearingly attractive young friend. But Maurice begins to suspect that Alec is planning to blackmail him and feels wretchedly sick as a result. He decides to leave Pendersleigh, and Alec and their burgeoning romance.

Talking to Clive as he drives his ailing friend to the train station, Maurice asks about Alec's background and what sort of a person he is. Clive, first noting that Alec comes across negatively as "smart," elaborates, "Um, wasn't his father the butcher at Osmington?"

In sharp contrast to hidebound Maurice's background checks, Alec writes yearningly and commandingly to his new lover while sitting in the boathouse, alone, waiting for Maurice to join him there.

Pretend to the other gentlemen that you want a stroll. It's easily managed. Then come down to the boathouse. Dear sir, let me share with you once before leaving old England. It's not asking too much.

The image of Alec alone in the boathouse – no one else present anywhere – writing a letter to Maurice extends the theme of lonely longing from Maurice to Alec. Just as Maurice wrote letters Clive refused to answer, Alec writes a letter to Maurice that he will not answer. As with Maurice's letters to Clive, we hear Alec's voiceover reading of his letter. Maurice does not answer Alec's letter given his fears that Alec is blackmailing him. Nevertheless, Alec's words initiating sex reverberate in Maurice's mind ("I know, sir. I know, sir. Come on."). Ivory is the master of the evocative voiceover. Alec's voiceover makes us privy to his interiority and makes him a subject, which is to say a subject of desire. The cyclical quality of letters sent from one man to another that receive no response threatens to embed these new lovers in the same impasse that blocked Maurice and Clive's connection. The solitary figure of Alec in the boathouse conveys decades, centuries, of the deep loneliness of queer desire.

Maurice, in their second session, informs Lasker Jones – in response to his complaint that Maurice is fighting him and now less suggestible than before – that he and Alec have been together, have "united," as the hypnotist puts it. Lasker Jones advises Maurice to relocate to France or Italy, "where homosex-

Figure 33
"Dear sir, let me share with you once before leaving old England." Alec writes
to Maurice telling him they should meet in the boathouse.

uality is no longer criminal," reminding Maurice that his kind were once put
to death in England. "England has always been disinclined," weighs in the
hypnotist, "to accept human nature."

Maurice shows Lasker Jones Alec's letter, which Maurice tells him to read
as evidence of blackmail assisted by an accomplice. We hear the rest of Alec's
letter read by the hypnotist:

> I, since cricket match, do long to place both arms around you and share
> with you. The above now seems sweeter than words can say. Mind and
> write if you don't come, for I get no sleep waiting. So come without fail
> to boathouse ... Pendersleigh, tomorrow night. Yours respectfully, Alec
> Scudder. Gamekeeper to C. Durham, Esquire.

Is it possible that these tender, ardent words, losing none of their plangency even in the hypnotist's pinched monotone, could really be taken for those of a blackmailer? Can't Maurice link these words to the clearly passionate love-making he and Alec shared? In any event, he does not. Lasker Jones, unlike the contemporary conversion-therapy guru hellbent on success, treats the matter in a measured way, and does not encourage Maurice to think the worst of Alec.

Alec's words echo Maurice's concerned, bereft ones to Clive when he was in Greece: "Clive, I'm so worried at not hearing from you. I get no sleep worrying." These pages passed from hand to hand, to evoke the title of a gay literary anthology co-edited by David Leavitt, unite the lovers here (for whom uniting poses such difficulties) and to lovers in history.

One thinks once again of Melville, and the themes of connection, disconnection, and isolation in his masterly 1853 tale "Bartleby, the Scrivener." Forster wrote about Melville's homoerotic masterpiece *Billy Budd, Sailor* (1891) as a critic, and co-wrote the libretto for Benjamin Britten's 1951 opera based on Melville's novella. As noted, Wilby, with his blond hair like Terence Stamp's in Peter Ustinov's 1962 film version and sturdy physicality, could have played the Handsome Sailor Billy Budd easily. Ivory's casting makes Maurice a contemporary Billy Budd. And both he and Forster make Melville a chief intertext in their depictions of male relations.

After the odd, off-putting Bartleby dies in the Tombs, a New York City prison, the narrator, a Wall Street lawyer, learns key information about his former employee Bartleby, best known for his singular phrase "I prefer not to." Bartleby was the lawyer's copyist, but he once worked in the Dead Letters Office. Forster, who knew Melville's work well, seems to be writing about dead letters, too – dead letters between men who find no way to honour Forster's *Howards End* dictate "only connect." "Bartleby" is a tale of failed male friendship thematized by "Dead Letters" that Bartleby once laboured over and that symbolize "dead men." Maurice and Alec verge on repeating the futile pattern.

Maurice returns to his stockbroking firm at Hill & Hall. Suddenly, Alec appears. Maurice, still convinced that he is being blackmailed, beholds his visitor with alarm. Things do not go well. Alec, having made every effort to be presentable, extends his hand to Maurice and calls him by his name, but Maurice does not shake his hand. (This moment echoes Maurice's class breach when he ill-advisedly extended his hand to Mrs Durham on first meeting her.) Maurice's nosy work colleagues gather around him and Alec, and Maurice quite cuttingly refers to Alec as Scudder, taking him by the arm and leading him out.

"You shouldn't treat me like a dog," Alec protests once they are out of doors. Incensed at Maurice's coldly cautious and classist treatment of him, he grows angry: "You said call me Maurice, but you never even wrote to me." He starts threatening Maurice. Nevertheless, the two men walk together to the British Museum.

Inside the museum, they share an unguarded moment of childlike pleasure when admiring the large-scale winged Assyrian lions (sometimes referred to as bulls, as does Forster in the novel [222]). According to the British Museum website, "Visit Rooms 6a and 6b to see two colossal winged human-headed lions that flanked an entrance to the royal palace of King Ashurnasirpal II (883–859 BC) at Nimrud. Plus, see a gigantic standing lion that stood at the entrance to the nearby Temple of Ishtar, the goddess of war." Marvelling at the "wonderful machinery to make a thing like that" this ancient culture must have possessed, Alec beams at Maurice, who offers an extremely welcoming reaction.

Both Forster and the film foreground these towering Assyrian art works rather than, say, the Winckelmannian classical male figure. In the novel, they pause "in the corridor of Roman emperors," but clearly not for long (220). The implication seems to be that the looming, man-faced lions represent a break from homo-Hellenism, an alternative tradition that speaks to queer desire, a different path to affiliation and tradition. As each man stands next to his lion, each finds himself mythologically represented by an exotic godlike, human-beast creature, and both find themselves doubled by a mythic same-sex couple in the sculptured pair.

But the rancour returns, and Alec warns his disappointing would-be lover, "It won't do, Mr Hall. I know what you're trying to do. You've had your fun. Now you've gotta pay up." Graves does not hold back from making Alec seem dislikable here, even menacing. Maurice's paranoid treatment of Alec as a blackmailer turns him into one, at least into someone who threatens blackmail.

Disrupting the volatile, tense atmosphere is a surprise appearance by Mr Ducie, Maurice's old schoolmaster who drew the male and female sex organs on the sand to instruct the child Maurice. He correctly recognizes his former pupil but flubs his name. "You're – you're Wimbleby, yes?" Maurice shifts gears and makes the consciously absurd statement, "My name's Scudder." Wilby has a wonderfully mild expression on his face as he utters this disarmingly, disorientingly facetious line. Alec corrects him and identifies himself as the bearer of this name, adding, provocatively, "I've got a serious charge to bring against *this* gentleman." They thoroughly discombobulate the harumphing Ducie, who is called back by his wife, standing with their children (an illustration of the life that Ducie instructed Maurice to acquire).

But then Alec has a change of heart. He says apologetically, "I shan't trouble you any further." Maurice, however, has become angry: "By God, if you'd split on me to Ducie, I'd have broken you … The police always back my sort against yours." This is all going as grindingly wrong as possible.

The two men walk outside in the rain, Alec under Maurice's large umbrella. Gradually, the atmosphere cedes to Alec's gentler complaints: "It rained even harder than this at the boathouse. It was even *colder*." Maurice explains that he was "frightened," and that Alec allowed himself to get frightened of Maurice, and that is why they are trying to "down each other." In response, Alec says – reveals – "I wouldn't take a penny from you. I don't want to hurt your little finger." That last line ranks amongst the tenderest in any film. "Come on," Alec continues, words he used when ravishing Maurice. "Let's give over

Figure 34
Ivory doubles Maurice and Alec, at odds in the British Museum, about to be
approached by Ducie.

talking." At this he takes Maurice's hand in his, and the two men stand together, facing one another, under the umbrella in the rain, an almost inex-
pressibly romantic image. Alec then daringly asks Maurice to share with him
once more, before he leaves for Argentina the next day. Maurice initially balks,
fumbling over the formal business dinner he must attend. But Alec presses
on, and the two do indeed share another night together.

The postcoital morning scene between Maurice and Alec ups the ante in
terms of queer representation by giving us images of the men naked and male
full-frontal nudity. It reveals more than the first such scene between them did,
which showed them bare-chested under covers. Nevertheless, this second such
scene of male-male intimacy somehow feels less naked than the first, perhaps
because the characters are at odds, their vulnerability what is chiefly denuded.

The hotel room has two beds in it, and the men lie together in one bed, talking *in medias res*. Ivory commences the scene by showing us the men's clothes, highly charged emblems of "homosexuality and heritage," as Richard Dyer puts it, laid out on the bed opposite theirs. The bodyless clothing bespeaks a kind of melancholic detachment, perhaps because it has been laid out with some neatness on the bed rather than left scattered on the floor and therefore redolent of hasty and rampant passions.

Alec complains about Mrs Durham's gorgonlike qualities and treatment of him, imitating her posh accent harshly: "'Oh, would you most kindly of your goodness post this for me? What's your name?'" He brazenly calls her "the old bitch." He then roughly teases Maurice about his sternness regarding the five-shilling tip that Alec had not accepted earlier, which seemed to Maurice at the time like Alec's conceited pique. (The Helena Bonham Carter character at the cricket match notes that she believes Alec to be a conceited man.) Alec had refused the tip not because of its inadequacy but because he did not want to take money from Mr Hall. Now, Alec imitates Maurice's earlier stern tones, which makes Maurice smile.

Alec climbs on top of Maurice and kisses and embraces him roughly, saying that Maurice will "remember that at least." The conversation turns to Alec's imminent emigration by boat to Argentina, a future devised for him by his older brother. Alec stands half-clothed before Maurice, naked below the waist as Maurice, seated on the bed, wraps his arms around Alec's waist. "You mean that you and I shan't meet again after now?" Maurice quietly asks. Alec, putting on a show of indifference, responds, "That's right. You got it quite correct." The tenderness of their intimacy makes the pessimistic place they have gotten to all the more sorrowful.

Maurice then comes up with a bold plan. He tells Alec not to go on the trip, to stay with him instead. "Miss my boat? Are you daft? Of all the bloody rubbish," Alec retorts, adding that Maurice sounds like a man who has never had to worry about a job or money. But Maurice presses on, saying that they've been given a rare opportunity in meeting one another; "You know it," he reminds Alec. Alec protests that Maurice can't possibly give up his city job, "what gives you money and position."

Maurice has been giving us signs of his surprisingly rebellious spirit all along, and now this spirit fully manifests itself. He tells Alec: "You can do anything once you know what it is. We can live without money, without people. We can live without position. We're not fools. We're both strong. There'll be someplace we could go." One thinks of the ill-fated heterosexual romance between Newland Archer and the American heiress Countess Ellen Olenska, *The Age of Innocence*, Edith Wharton's 1920 novel adapted by Martin Scorsese and Jay Cocks for Scorsese's great 1993 film. In the film, when Newland encourages the Countess to run away with him and from their impossible predicament, she sadly refuses. Reflecting on the social strictures that keep them apart, she asks him where they could go to be freed of them: "Do you know such a country?"

Essentially, this is also Alec's response to Maurice: "It wouldn't work, Maurice. It would be the ruin of us both." Alec sits beside Maurice now. Rupert Graves's consistently amazing performance as Alec, full of seismic shifts in emphasis, oscillations between cheekiness and fervent directness, decisiveness and fuzzy uncertainty, reaches its height here. Alec, now fully clothed, sits on the bed beside Maurice as he tells him his plan won't work. Graves pauses midway through this sentence and emphasizes the last word: "It would be the ruin ... of us *both*." Alec might be cautioning Maurice to save himself or reminding Maurice that Alec will be jeopardized no less than he: the complexities are rich, thanks to Graves's finely modulated interpretation, a moving match for Wilby's nuanced and attentive one.

Ivory has a Hitchcock-like knack for making small, enclosed spaces fluidly mobile. (I am thinking of what Hitchcock does with the nearly single-set *Dial M for Murder* especially, and of course *Rope*, another film about the horrors of the closet. And now that we mention this, one might consider two actors in *Maurice* from *Frenzy*, which Hitchcock made in England, Barry Foster and Billie Whitelaw.) The scene commences with a slow, steady track-in showing the clothes-strewn bed; then the camera shifts so that we can see the men in their bed on the opposite side. A kind of decorum, perhaps, is indicated by this distanced view of the men in bed. But it provides a striking contrast to the intimate shots of them in bed in the Russet Room, where we are practically imparadised, to wax Miltonic, in their arms.

Maurice and Alec verge on never meeting again. Ivory's camera moves as if it were weightless and unconstrained, smoothly alternating between shots of Maurice on the bed, seated, and Alec standing opposite him as he dresses. In two extraordinary medium shots after Alec has told Maurice his plan won't work, Alec looks at himself in a small mirror above the washbasin as he washes his face and smooths his floppy dark hair. Reflected in the mirror is not only his face but, on the left-hand side, Maurice's head, albeit from the back. Ivory upends the formal nature of the single shot ("dirties" it, in industry parlance) by including Maurice's image in the mirror, making this a two shot. This stylized image provides an exquisite expression of the men's simultaneous intimacy (their faces captured in the same frame) and disconnection (their inability to face one another).

In the second peculiar two shot, the mirror that captures Alec's face also captures Maurice's, but he now looks into the mirror as well. These contrasting mirror images, the back of Maurice's head, the next of Maurice looking at Alec and at us, provide visual commentary on the emotional currents of the tense but sombre scene: the first indicates a remove, an impasse; the second a silent imploring. As Alec moves away from the mirror, he stares into it, and the face that stares back at him is Maurice's, as if he were Alec's true reflection. The painterly quality of Ivory's camera framing and compositions – these shots could be framed and hung in a museum – provides not prettification but pointed interpretation.

Now fully dressed and leaving the room, Alec remarks, "Pity we ever met, really, if you think about it." Endearingly, but also an indication of their class divide, Alec confirms that he won't be interrogated at the front desk since Maurice has paid for the room. "You'll be all right," Maurice says, resignedly.

Figure 35
Alec stares into the mirror, and Maurice's face stares back at him, as if he were
Alec's true reflection.

Maurice heads to the docks to see Alec off in the next scene. A police officer
sees the gentleman wandering about uncertainly and comes up to help him
and points out the Scudders' boat. Maurice lives in a world of money and position, as Alec rightly noted, and it means that those in the labouring classes
look after him.

Yet in climbing aboard the boat and interacting with the Scudders, Maurice,
well-dressed and looking the part of the gentleman, looks unsure and out of
place, subject to attack. Alec's aged, shabby-genteel parents (Olwen Griffiths
plays his mother and Alan Whybrow his father) look at him with confusion
and, in the father's case especially, suspicion. Alec's cocky older brother Fred
(Christopher Hunter) is as slick and brusque as can be. Will Maurice be outed,
terrible epithets hurled at him?

Suddenly, Reverend Borenius appears, telling Maurice how much he admires his charity toward Alec. Borenius's appearance adds to the tense, suspicious atmosphere. He explains how fearful he is that Alec will not be confirmed or maintain his religious faith. Alec, the reverend fears, has been guilty of sensuality and fornication. After a beat, he says, "with women." (There is a deleted scene on the Blu-ray edition of the film showing Alec sporting sensually with two chambermaids at Pendersleigh, and pausing his frolics because Maurice is looking at him.)

The unthinkable happens. Alec does not show up for his boat. The others begin to panic, but Maurice begins beaming, and Robbins's score turns its notes to hopeful ones. Alec has missed his boat because he has decided to stay in England and be with Maurice, who intuits this.

Before moving on to the last section of the film, I want to underscore the significance of Simcox and, perhaps, Reverend Borenius as closeted characters. Simcox and Borenius invert – if you will – one another, Simcox seeming very much aware of the nature of his desire for Alec, Borenius a stranger to his, sublimating it into ceaseless efforts to save Alec's soul. Indeed, Suzanne Speidel, in her invaluable study of *Maurice*'s work-in-progress scripts, reports that it was Ruth Prawer Jhabvala who made the suggestion that Simcox "uses his authority over Alec to vent his frustrated physical desire for him" (Speidel 2014, 304).

The snide Simcox is the most purely negative character in the film, insinuating secret knowledge of Clive's and Maurice's proclivities. When Risley is convicted, Simcox brings his master the paper, mock-concernedly asking Clive if he knew Risley while impugning Risley's behaviour. Clive sharply rebukes the servant never to discuss such matters again. As we have noted, Simcox, his prohibitive eye unerring, spies on Clive and Maurice embracing at the ancestral home the Goblin House one morning. He expertly, under the cover of servile concern and propriety, notices and points out the mud tracks on the carpet in Maurice's room the morning after he and Alec first make love, and he also points out the ladder outside the Russet Room window, the stairway to heaven in need of immediate removal. It should be added, of course, that, like Alec and Milly, the maid, Simcox is a servant. Though he seems rather threatening, Simcox represents an exploited class.

For his part, Reverend Borenius insistently monitors Alec's behaviour, enlisting Mrs Durham's support in about getting Alec confirmed in the church (or, better put, impressing upon her the utter necessity that he do so). Borenius's presence on the Argentina-bound boat, ostensibly to pass along letters of introduction on Alec's behalf to an Argentinian bishop, signals his devotion to the young man that he most likely desires but cannot access on any level save the most churchly. In the novel, Maurice seethes with animosity toward Borenius; in Ivory's version, the reverend is a more wan, loveless presence, especially as faithfully portrayed by Eyre.

Maurice makes his way to Pendersleigh. It is evening, suffused with the light from "the last dying of the day" as in the novel (240). In the novel, Maurice's presence is announced to Clive by Simcox. The film eliminates this bit of business. Like a misplaced Romeo, Maurice calls up from ground level to Clive, who has emerged from a room where others have gathered and is standing on a balcony, practising a political speech. No Juliet he.

On the ground, Clive playfully – or fake-playfully – bops his friend on the head with the speech, and continues to get everything wrong, convincing himself that Maurice's news is his engagement to the woman Anne suspects him of wooing. Clive encourages Maurice to stay over and speak to Anne about this, talking to a woman about such matters always being best. "I'm not here to see Anne," Maurice says sharply. "Or you, Clive. It's miles worse for you. I'm in love with Alec Scudder." Ivory frames the men in a medium two-shot, Clive seated on a bench in his customary tuxedo, Maurice in a long trench coat and wearing a hat, one leg propped up on the bench. He looks poised, ready to spring.

Clive's response to Maurice's declaration of love for Alec, given after Clive has risen from the bench and moved to a more discreet, standing distance, is so arch as to be almost bravura: "What a grotesque announcement."

This final confrontation between Maurice and Clive ends their relationship as it fires up Maurice's new one. Clive protests the sexual nature of Maurice's relationship with Alec – hasn't Maurice learned anything yet? "The sole excuse for any relationship between two men is that it remain purely Platonic," Clive insists. Maurice responds defiantly and protectively, "I've shared with Alec." "Shared what?" Clive asks. "Everything. Alec slept with me in the Russet Room when you and Anne were away. Also in town." Clive is horrified ("Good God!"), but Maurice has made something clear to him: "I'm flesh and blood, Clive, if you'll condescend to such low things."⁹

Maurice reminds Clive that he kissed his hand, a reference that Clive sharply rebukes: "Don't allude to that!" Maurice makes it clear to his former friend and would-be lover that their relationship has come to an end. When Clive demands, "May I ask if you intend to pursue –," Maurice cuts him off right away: "No. No, you may not ask. I'll tell you everything up to this minute, but not a word beyond." By this point, the men stand side by side, and now Ivory frames them in a medium two-shot close-up that grants them equal prominence. Importantly, it grants Maurice prominence as a sexual agent and, finally, Clive's rhetorical match.

As shot, Wilby/Maurice looks heroically handsome in his period attire while Grant/Clive looks desexualized, pale, pinched, his hair slicked back in an androgynous manner as if he were a boy or a girl playing a mustachioed man in a family theatrical. They are outdoors at night, but no romance or mystery or sexual heat suffuses the scene. It's tonally and compositionally apt as these failed lovers' final exchange and as Maurice's decisive break from his mendacious mentor.

With a spring in his step, Maurice makes his way speedily across the grounds, Robbins's score sounding buoyantly anticipatory. Maurice's entrance into the greenwood is the literal and symbolic domain of Forster's radical romantic vision. At one point, Maurice takes his long coat off and carries it on his arm, a subtle signal that Maurice is paring down his citified armor and becoming one with his environment, and a more prosaic indication of the overwarming length of the passage from Clive's residence to the boathouse. (The novel makes it clear that Maurice also walked from the train station to Penge.)

Maurice enters the boathouse, only to find the interior empty and silent, devoid of Alec. The dying natural light emphasizes the boathouse's barrenness, the boats lying listlessly before him. Seen in wide shot, Maurice stands before us in his entirety, and looks unspeakably alone. The crepuscular shadows on the wall give the image a horror movie ambiance. He plops his coat in one of the boats, continuing his literal and thematic shedding of skins. Suddenly, he sees a door. Since 1939, no one has been able to open a door in the cinema unmomentously. Our Dorothy of gay romance now opens the door to reveal the warmest colours, a darkened private chamber, lit from within by the glow of a lit fireplace, where Alec lies sleeping, his backside invitingly poised, waiting for him. Alec sleepily but sweetly asks, "So you got the wire, then? ... Telling you to come here to the boathouse at Pendersleigh without fail." Maurice did not receive the wire, but he didn't need to. He embraces Alec, scooping him from the ground and holding him fast, and they kiss passionately. Love has superseded dead letters.

Alec says, his lips sensually moist and sensually affixed to his lover's ear, "Now we shan't never be parted. It's finished." As Graves delivers the line, we hear, "It's *finished*." Maurice kisses Alec on the lips, twice, more softly and tenderly now, the two entwined men lit up by the chiaroscuro glow of the fireplace. The scene is shot like an oil painting, a Caravaggesque tableau, perhaps a nod from one great gay visual artist to another. An over-the-shoulder shot of Maurice's wonderstruck, palpably grateful face as he embraces Alec – intensely, for dear life, like shipwrecked survivors – concludes the scene. "We'll meet in your boathouse yet," Maurice promised, and he was right. The movie, like Forster, gives gay men their happy ending, a hard-won and exhilarating one.

Forster was invested in giving his heroes this hopeful closure, but this happy ending has been widely debated. Alec's conclusion-making words to Maurice, "Now we shan't never be parted. It's finished" (in the novel, "And now we shan't be parted no more, and that's finished" [240]), achingly contrast with our historical knowledge (which Forster discussed) of the imminence of the First World War, which will break out in July 1914, not a full year after Maurice and Alec come together as lovers who "shan't never be parted." Decades of speculation about the lovers' fate have occurred (see Monk 2020). These enduring questions deepen the bittersweet significance of the happy ending.

Adaptation Matters

Clive, however, remains stuck liminally between nostalgia and reality. Back in his bedroom after saying goodnight to Simcox, he commences nighttime rituals. He puts his arms around Anne, seated before the mirror on her vanity table, his head on her shoulders. Their eyes lock as they hold their gaze in the mirror, but then Clive averts his eyes, leading her to look at him with alarm. She continues to do so even as he walks away and begins fastening wooden shutters, throwing her a courteous smile. His attempt to maintain his social, marital façade fails, however, when he pauses at one window and stares out at the darkened grounds. We now see what Clive sees in his mind, the image of Maurice when they were at university together, a hale, handsome, cheerful blond fellow on the green playfully waving at someone, presumably the unseen younger Clive.

Interviewed at the time of the film's release, James Wilby discussed his character input, which "exceeded his mere enacting of it. Maurice's poignant gesture of farewell, which is intercut into the film's final scene, was done at Wilby's insistence. 'In one tiny flash it sends the audience right back to reexperience the whole film,' he proudly says of the brief but effective moment" (Hachem 1987, 64). It is to Wilby's credit that he envisioned this moment, and to Ivory's that he realized the vision.

This last sequence reverses the cinematographic effects of the previous one with Ivory's characteristic visual irony. As we have noted, the film reverses the

Figure 36
"Now we shan't never be parted. It's finished." Maurice, with Alec in the boathouse at last, contemplates his beloved.

order of the novel's last two scenes, having Maurice's final conversation with Clive occur before his reunion with Alec. But the film, like the novel, ends with Clive, reflecting on his relationship with the forever departed Maurice. The film, then, has two final sequences, the first being Maurice's discovery of Alec in the boathouse, the second Clive's nighttime window-shutting and memory theatre. Ivory pairs these final sequences and contrasts them, a conscious chiasmus. Maurice's disappointing inspection of the empty boathouse illuminated by crepuscular light leads to his ardently fulfilling entrance into the fireplace-lit chamber where Alec, love, and possibility await. Reversing this chromatic trajectory, Clive stares out at night from his shadowy bedroom, partially illuminated by a lamp, into the darkness of night, which suddenly transforms into a daylit vista where Maurice, forever young, beckons, a brightness that can only exist in memory. Robbins's romantic score intensifies this surge of feeling as Clive envisions and memorializes the friend he loved and rejected and has now lost. Anne rises and comes over to Clive, placing her hand on his right shoulder and perching her head on the left. Concerned, she asks her husband, "Who were you talking to?" He lies to her, with another courteous smile: "No one. I was just trying out a speech." He turns his face to Anne as the movie and his desire fade to black.

"To the end of his life Clive was not sure of the exact moment of departure," the narrator observes in the novel about Maurice's absence from Clive's life. "Out of some external Cambridge his friend began beckoning to him, clothed in the sun, and shaking out the scents and sounds of the May term" (246). Ivory's cinema, and Hugh Grant's performance, exquisitely captures this evanescent and infinite mnemonic effect. One can rewatch the final moments again and again and find new resonances. Clive seems sympathetic as he looks back at Anne, accepting her love. Or Clive looks sinister in his mendacity. Or Clive looks stricken by loss. It's a richly suggestive image.

Deleted Scenes

Available on the Cohen Media Blu-ray and on the Merchant Ivory Collection DVD, several deleted scenes provide a glimpse into the filmmaking process. I am generally of the belief that filmmakers delete scenes for a reason; see, for example, the coda for *Vertigo* (1958) that Hitchcock was required to film in order to appease the classical Hollywood production code. In the thankfully removed coda, Scotty (James Stewart) and Midge (Barbara Bel Geddes) pensively listen to a radio news broadcast announcing that the villain Gavin Elster (Tom Helmore) has been apprehended in Europe, an ending that cancels out the theatrical release's magnificent final shot of Scotty staring down at the fallen Judy (Kim Novak) from the top of the church bell tower. That said, some of the scenes and moments that Ivory cut out from *Maurice* are truly missed.

As noted in the previous chapter, the principal excisions are scenes portraying two characters who do not appear in the final film: the Hall sisters' friend Gladys Olcott (Serena Gordon), whom Maurice unwisely and hurtfully makes a pass at in the novel, and Dickie Barry (Adrian Ross Magenty), the nephew of Dr Barry, with whom Maurice becomes infatuated.

Several other key moments can be found among the deleted scenes. There is a long sequence at Clive Durham's London flat, where Maurice spends the night, before Clive departs for Greece; the first night of their lovemaking has Maurice and Alec exchange postcoital words not included in the film. In my view, these scenes and those involving Dickie should have been included in the final cut.

Forster renders the scene where Maurice makes a pass at Gladys a chillingly effective indictment of the closet and its misogynistic repercussions, as we have discussed. But the encounter comes across limply in the film's deleted scene, which oddly portrays Gladys as the initiator of romantic intent. She gauchely tries and fails to kiss Maurice as he instructs her in the art of forming cigarette smoke-rings when she exhales. Forster's version of Gladys is tougher and more resilient: she rebuffs Maurice's palpably insincere attempts to woo her, whereas the film's version depicts her as painfully embarrassed when rebuffed by him.

The teenage Dickie Barry stays with the Halls after Maurice and Clive have had their terrible falling out after Clive returns from Greece. Dickie has been given Maurice's bedroom, and he has been relegated to the attic. At the behest of his querulous sister Kitty, Maurice goes up to Dickie's room to wake him up for breakfast. When Maurice peers into the room, he sees a naked Dickie, asleep and sprawled out on the bed. The shot of the slumbering Dickie in all his posterior glory is as beautiful as any in the Merchant Ivory canon. Wilby conveys the complexity of Maurice's responses, which we can describe as surprised by lust.

Clearly, the filmmakers got cold feet about depicting Maurice as being sexually interested in a teenager, an anticipation of the plot of *Call Me by Your Name*. The scenes between Wilby and Adrian Ross Magenty, later cast by Ivory as the effete Tibby Schlegel in *Howards End*, brim with an intriguing nervous energy, as Maurice awkwardly flirts with the lad and Dickie reservedly holds back but at times appears seducible. Given that the film is an exploration of the lived experience of the closet, these scenes add considerably to our understanding of Maurice's ongoing predicament of sexual longing, loneliness, and estrangement.

A particular loss is the sequence at Clive's London flat. Maurice regularly stays over with Clive on Wednesday nights after evenings of dinner and drink, but this time Clive – shaken by Risley's sentencing – attempts to dissuade Maurice from staying over. The two have a tense exchange at the flat as Clive tries to confront Maurice about the feelings Clive has "stirred up" in him, and Maurice retreats from the looming row, finally seeking refuge in his room.

In one of the most striking shots Ivory ever created, the naked Maurice rises from his bed and stares at himself in a full-length mirror. It's a shot worthy of Rainer Werner Fassbinder. Maurice seems to be staring at his beautiful body, untouched, unfulfilled, in hopes of answers for his sexual and emotional deprivation. Later, restless, moody Clive surprisingly asks to get into bed with Maurice (both men clothed), and Maurice embraces him. Might some sexual contact and release finally occur? Not a chance. Clive curtly responds that this isn't helping, either, and promptly vacates the bed, disengaging from his pining, hungry friend.

Other deleted scenes involve Alec. Maurice first sees the gamekeeper in a greenhouse with Milly the maid and her female cousin, flirting with them as they all suck down stolen grapes. The visual exchange between Alec and Maurice palpably conveys an erotic *frisson* even as Maurice's look also imparts judgment on Alec and the girls' misbehaviour. Another theme that Forster develops but the movie does not: Maurice's envy at Alec's casual bisexuality, not hinted at in the film, his ability to marry a woman and father a child should he wish to do so.

The glorious first postcoital morning between Maurice and Alec is beautifully rendered in the film. Nevertheless, it is a pity that the scene preceding it was cut. As Earl G. Ingersoll discusses,

As the scene moves toward morning, viewers are being shown the brief vignette of Simcox outside the house, scrutinizing the ladder propped against the dining room roof just outside Maurice's bedroom window … When the film jumps ahead abruptly from predawn to bright morning sunlight and Maurice is atop Alec, holding him down at the shoulders, Alec addresses his bed partner as "Sir." Daylight and their discussion of the upcoming cricket match impel Alec to begin acknowledging their imminent return to their public personae. Maurice's forceful repetition here of his own first name to reestablish the intimacy of the night world leaves the impression of an elided conversation, and the paratext confirms that there was one. As a result what was rendered in the uncut scene as lovemaking is at risk of being reduced to a chance sexual encounter, although the film scene does end with Maurice's question: "Alec, did you ever dream you had a friend, someone to last your whole life?" Ivory expresses misgivings about having deleted a brief section of the conversation between Alec and Maurice, after they have made love. Associating the scene with Maurice's question, "May I ask your name?" the director is clearly regretful to have lost the scene: "There would have been room and should've been room for Maurice's renewal of desire." Ivory's regretful tone suggests he cannot recall why he deleted the scene. (Ingersoll 2012, 151)

Including these scenes would have made a great film all the richer. One of the losses of this cut scene is Alec's description of Maurice when he first saw him, eating the purloined grapes: "I did think that you looked at me angry and gentle, both together."

Chapter 4

"Did You Ever Dream You Had a Friend?": *Maurice*, Reception, Queer Theory

"Did you ever dream you'd a friend, Alec? Nothing else but just 'my
friend,' he trying to help you and you him. A friend," he repeated,
sentimental suddenly. "Someone to last your whole life and you his.
I suppose such a thing can't really happen outside sleep." (197)

Maurice speaks these postcoital words to Alec in Forster's novel, and they are
repeated, to a certain extent, in the film: "Did you ever dream you had a friend,
someone to last your whole life?" Maurice's body lies atop Alec's on the morning after they have first made love, and Maurice asks these questions in the
spirit of someone who has finally quenched a longstanding thirst and can
hardly believe his relief.

The film tropes the term "friend" throughout. "I could hardly believe my
eyes when I saw you among his friends here," Reverend Borenius exclaims
when encountering Maurice on the boat meant to take Alec to Argentina.
Maurice comically chafes when Anne tells him he's "the eighth friend of
Clive's" she's spoken to about their engagement. Maurice falsely accuses Ada
of trying to seduce Clive: "You have the satisfaction of breaking up our friendship at least." Reassuring his mother that there was nothing questionable about
his kissing the prostrate Clive on the mouth, Maurice reminds her, "As you

Figure 37
Friends of friends and lovers: James Ivory and Ismail Merchant in 1975.
Internet image.

know, we're great friends." Friendship comes up significantly in the dean's
class on *The Phaedrus*: "The loved one" grows used "to being near his friend."

As a breakthrough film in gay representation, *Maurice* begins a dialogue
that isn't taken up again until close to two decades later, in Ang Lee's film
Brokeback Mountain (2005), which was based on the short story by Annie
Proulx published in the *New Yorker* (6 October 1997). In the film, Jack Twist
(Jake Gyllenhaal) gets back in touch with his now-married lover Ennis Del
Mar (Heath Ledger) by writing him a brief postcard that addresses Ennis as
"Friend." One of the songs on the soundtrack is Willie Nelson's achingly sad
elegy, "He Was a Friend of Mine":

He was a friend of mine
Every time I think of him
I just can't keep from cryin'
'Cause he was a friend of mine

It may sound "sentimental suddenly" to say this, but for many of us, movies like *Maurice* were our friends in a time when they were few in the larger culture. In my closeted teen and early college days, *Maurice*, as *A Room with a View* and *The Bostonians* had also done, spoke the language of my own desire before even I could articulate it. That I also consider it a great film deepens the connection. I have been stunned to encounter such hostility to works like *Maurice* and *Brokeback*, especially from gay and queer critics. To address such criticism and clarify why I view Merchant Ivory's *Maurice* as a salutary achievement, I turn to two essays, one written shortly after *Maurice* premiered, and one that makes mention of *Maurice*, D.A. Miller's review of Luca Guadagnino's 2017 film *Call Me by Your Name*.

Reception and Reaction: The Response to *Maurice*

As I trust has been made clear, I dispute the classification of Merchant Ivory films as heritage cinema or costume drama when critics deploy these classifications as terms of abuse. For example, in her contemporaneous review in the English publication *The Listener*, Margaret Walters wrote, "The movie is intelligent and subtle … But the moments of authentic awkwardness and pain are swamped by the film's relentless good taste: even the things that were harsh and stultifying in pre-war England are bathed in a nostalgic glow. What was urgent and immediate for Forster has become costume drama, safely sealed off in the prettified past" (Walters 1987, 40). Pauline Kael's review, redolent of her attitudes toward Merchant Ivory, follows suit: "all we see is costumes and set decoration, mansions and grounds" (Kael 1989, 361). Though costume drama is a neutral term, it is not neutral when used as it is here, pejoratively. Ivory's painstaking attention to detail means to ground us in the period and the specific milieu, not to embalm the past and certainly not to enshrine a nostalgic view of it.

Ivory has repeatedly spoken of the poor response gay critics in the UK gave *Maurice* on its release. "When *Maurice* came out, there wasn't a single English critic who praised it wholeheartedly, even though every single one of them was gay. It is shocking to think back" on this, he comments (Freeman 2021). Perhaps the most succinct summary of the responses Ivory refers to was Alan Hollinghurst's review in the *Times Literary Supplement* of 1987, titled, in a phrase that says it all, "Suppressive Nostalgia." Hollinghurst, perhaps our greatest contemporary writer of gay fiction, would seem to be an inherently oppositional critic for Merchant Ivory, given the novelist's determined inclusion of graphic gay sex scenes in his mercilessly lyrical, acutely detailed work. (*The Swimming-Pool Library*, his landmark debut novel, would be published in 1988.) Nevertheless, Hollinghurst's criticisms that the film errs by not including the novel's key episodes of Maurice's attempted seduction of Gladys Olcott and sexual infatuation with the young Dickie Barry are well-taken. Given the general sense that the film did not impress gay community media commentators in its year of release, particularly in the UK, it is interesting to revisit US responses, which were decidedly wide-ranging.

Writing in Boston's *Gay Community News*, Michael Bronski echoed heritage-film criticism of Merchant Ivory in his evaluation that *Maurice*'s "romanticized style which relies heavily upon both good taste and a certain amount of visual and editing restraint ensures that Maurice is not a *hot* movie." He continues: "Yes, the boys are pretty (as is the furniture), and they do languidly touch." But even in their sexual intimacy, "it's hard to imagine that any of the characters have hard-ons" (Bronski 1987). Bronski does not evince much sensitivity to Ivory's style and the slow-burn accumulation of a passion that eventually breaks the dams of restraint.

In sharp contrast, Stephen Harvey, writing in the *Village Voice*, praised the film: "Ivory's calculated pacing and subtly subversive eye really pay their dramatic dividends." Maurice's affair with Alec, which can easily descend into self-parody, "is handled so shrewdly as to quell all potential titters." Ivory, in the critic's view, brings "considerable grace" to the material as well as "the astringency Forster couldn't bear to use himself." *Maurice* exceeds the achievement of *A Room with a View*; it is a "stimulating movie which actually improves on its distinguished source" (Harvey 1987). Mark Halleck, writing in the *New York Native*, called *Maurice* the "movie of the year … a classic homosexual love story" (Halleck 1987). And the gay-fiction writer and critic Christopher (Chris) Bram published a long, appreciative interview with Ivory and Ismail Merchant in the same issue.

Melodrama and Its Discontents

Mark Finch and Richard Kwietniowski's essay "Melodrama and *Maurice*: Homo Is Where the HET Is" was published in the leading film studies journal *Screen* in 1988. Though I disagree with some their views, their essay makes several salient points about *Maurice* as a melodrama for gay men. They provide more depth regarding the importance of genre than Hollinghurst does in his review. "The film plasters melodrama over something whose force is simpler and more psychological" (Hollinghurst 1987, 15).

The authors express surprise at discovering that the film "utilises a number of key constructions from Hollywood's most ambiguous site of wish-fulfilment, the melodrama: absent fathers, denial, alteration, illness, hysteria, tears, unrequited love, isolation, paranoia, entrapment, duplicity, false closure." It does so while inscribing Forster in the film text "as a voice of (gay) authenticity," the "unusually complete" screenplay adaptation establishing him as "the author of this Letter from an Unknown Invert." Finch and

Kwietniowski implicitly – and, given the tone of their riff on its title, derisively – link the film to Max Ophüls's great melodrama *Letter from an Unknown Woman* (1948), starring Joan Fontaine and Louis Jourdan. Indeed, gay men's associations with Hollywood melodrama are so entrenched that the film is "already massively over-determined" as a gay male object, given that "the subtext for a weepie is always homosexuality" (Finch and Kwietniowski 1988, 73).

The derisive tone steeps the initial sections of the essay, especially in its familiar recourse to criticisms of the heritage cinema tradition apparently embodied by Ivory's film: "*Maurice* is ... a literary adaptation, and a prestigious one at that, continuing another tradition peculiar to British cinema: plenty of words to be spoken, a structure dictated by drastic time shifts, and a certain faithfulness to the hallowed source"; being only "fourthly" about homosexuality, the film in art-cinema fashion "offers a respectable combination of psychology and titillation...of nubile youths, stiff upper collars ... a sublimation suitable for school-trips" (Finch and Kwietniowski 1988, 72–3).

The authors also make the debatable point that Clive emerges as the true, melodramatic subject of the film at its conclusion. "The film drags the narrative from the novel's uncomplicated utopianism to the familiar false closure of melodrama, but suddenly swerves (at last) into key focus on Clive and a loaded iconography: Clive bids Maurice farewell, steps back inside the (leaking) family home, past the knowing servant, bolts down the shutters, embraces his wife in front of a mirror, stands by the window and remembers/fantasises Maurice standing beneath him, shirt-tails flapping, on the college lawn. 'Come on, come on,' he urges, like Lisa's declaration in *Letter from an Unknown Woman*" (Finch and Kwietniowski 1988, 78–9).

If structural similarities exist between *Maurice* and melodrama that suggest Clive as the heroine who sacrificially renounces desire, surely one's experience of the film does not bear out this schema. Our allegiance has not shifted to Clive, nor have our sympathies in the main. This moment of indelible poignancy, Clive's suddenly memory-charged gaze, reminds us of the bond that existed between Clive and Maurice and more than hints that he was and remains Clive's true, lingering love. Indeed, despite the way that Finch and Kwietniowski frame *Maurice* as fourthly, i.e., lastly, interested in homosexuality (which they describe coyly early on as *le vice anglais*), these final shots seem, to me, the clearest statement made by the film that the closet shrivels up not only desire but the emotional life generally. Maurice can only exist as Clive's bittersweet memory, incompatible with his closeted life.

One of the most interesting readings the critics offer is that of the sinister servant Simcox as "close cousin to woman's picture archetype Mrs Danvers," who oversees the staff at the grand manor Manderley in Hitchcock's first American film, *Rebecca* (1940). Played by Dame Judith Anderson, Mrs Danvers is widely regarded as one of the most prominent lesbian characters in classical Hollywood cinema, albeit a negative portrait. Preying on the innocent un-named heroine (Joan Fontaine) newly married to the enigmatic, aloof millionaire Maxim de Winter (Laurence Olivier), Danvers maintains a fanatical devotion to the dead first wife, the titular figure whom Danvers clearly still loves and ardently desires. Simcox, in contrast, works through subtle, insinuating hints at the depravity of his employers (Clive) and their circle (Maurice). His own sexuality remains hidden if implied as a self-hating one.

Finch and Kwietniowski's essay valuably outlines the importance of *Maurice's* connections to the woman's film/melodrama. The linkages among *Maurice, Brokeback Mountain,* and *Call Me by Your Name* proceed from this basis.[1] As films that elicit tears, they thematize deprivation while forging community precisely through the shared experience of loss. That *Maurice* is the only one of the three works with a healing happy ending places it in an ironic temporal relation to the works that follow it, clarifying and highlighting just how unusual Forster's vision of gay romantic possibilities remains.

Figure 38
Clive's memory image of Maurice at university.

No Sex, We're Queer: Miller and Leavitt on *Maurice*

D.A. Miller wrote one of the definitive queer theory film-related essays, "Anal Rope," on Hitchcock's 1948 film *Rope*. While his views on Hitchcock have considerably softened over the years, as evinced by his book *Hidden Hitchcock* (2016), which venerates the director as an endlessly fascinating prestidigitator (returning to pre-Chabrol and Rohmer views in the process), the 1990 "Anal Rope" burns with a fury that continues to scorch.

Miller painstakingly exposes what he claims are the homophobic qualities of Hitchcock's deeply peculiar, idiosyncratic, and, to my mind, both politically and aesthetically radical film. Chiefly, Miller focuses on the fact that the film

Figure 39
Though successfully heterosexual to the public world, Clive continues to desire
Maurice in his memories.

famously seems devoid of any cuts. What is cut out of the film, in Miller's
view, is the homosexual desire that ostensibly inheres in this tale, loosely inspired by the infamous Leopold and Loeb case and adapted from Patrick
Hamilton's play, of gay lovers in a swanky Manhattan apartment who murder
a friend of theirs for the pleasure of feeling superior to him and perversely
throw a dinner party organized around his hidden corpse.[2]

As I have discussed elsewhere, even though I disagree with Miller's reading
of *Rope* as homophobic, I do appreciate the context for Miller's anger, the
early 1990s and the ongoing AIDS crisis before the development of protease
inhibitors, the fresh election of George H.W. Bush and the two terms, catas-
trophic for gay lives, of the Reagan presidency. Nevertheless, Miller established

a stance in this essay that can be taken as the baseline of Foucauldian gay-male-inflected queer theory from the 1980s to the present: it is axiomatic that commercial as well as art cinema is homophobic even at its most earnest.

Miller's brief mention of *Maurice* in his ideologically loaded pan of *Call Me by Your Name*, a film that links its screenwriter James Ivory to newer iterations of the problem as Miller sees it, decisively places it at the forefront of "an exasperating tradition" that strenuously distorts and obscures homosexual love, sex, and desire. This tradition, "begun by *Maurice* (1987) and continued with *Brokeback Mountain* (2005) and *Moonlight* (2016)," is located within "the mainstream gay-themed movie (or MGM)."

Miller argues that the MGM is defined by "three consistent objectives."

First, to elicit sympathy for gay male love in its struggle to affirm itself under the barbaric repressions of the closet. Second, to limit the visibility of gay male sex, whose depiction is scrupulously kept from approaching the explicitness reserved for hetero-consummations (which the MGM by no means dispenses with: the gay protagonists regularly pass through the bisexual antechamber). The synergy between these aims hardly needs to be stated. Only by averting our eyes from the distinctive gay male sex act can we defend a man's freedom to perform it; in the classically abstract liberal way, all is approved of on condition that nothing be looked at. More interesting is the MGM's third objective: to be a thing of beauty – beauty so overpowering, or overdone, that (provided the other objectives are met) it persuades viewers they are watching a masterpiece, "gay sex or not." This mandatory aesthetic laminate, which can never shine brightly enough with dappled light to win critical accolades, is a curious phenomenon. (Miller 2018)

Of the numerous ways that we might respond to Miller's critique, the immediately obvious question is, does it make any difference that some of the most prominent filmmakers in the MGM tradition of Miller's devising are themselves gay, namely Ismail Merchant, James Ivory, and Luca Guadagnino?

Another question follows swiftly on the first. Is Miller's critique breaking fresh ground, or does it largely reiterate the now hoary argument against heritage cinema, that it is a cinema of prettiness that embalms its subjects in nostalgic amber? By lumping together works like *Maurice* and *Call Me by Your Name*, set in the early 1980s and a neo-heritage film, Miller cordons off films that emphasize a humanist approach to love, sex, and desire as ideologically suspect and indeed worthless. There is also little difference, in the critic's view, between a film made during the height of the AIDS crisis and one made in a moment of radically visible sexual plurality, which is not to suggest the 2000s represent a halcyon era of sexual possibility but merely to note that our moment promotes the idea that sexuality and gender identity present a spectrum of options.

Echoing Miller, the novelist and short-story writer David Leavitt – one of the key figures of gay fiction to emerge in the Reagan 1980s – skewers *Maurice* the film in his otherwise graceful and informative introductory essay to the 2005 Penguin Classics publication of *Maurice*. Leavitt, whose great novel *The Lost Language of Cranes* (1986) compares the stories of a gay man and his closeted father, offers a welcome rebuttal to Cynthia Ozick's indefensibly hostile review of *Maurice* when it was posthumously published. But when it comes to Ivory's film, Leavitt loses all critical perspective.

The film of *Maurice* (1987) may be the greatest offense of all, so shorn is it of sexuality. Most tellingly, Merchant and Ivory cast the very blond James Wilby in the title role, even though Forster makes so very much of Maurice's hair being black. For Forster, black hair connotes virility; Maurice is dark, in part, because he is linked with the primordial eroticism of essential night. In a crucial scene, when he walks into the dining room at Penge with his head "all yellow with evening primrose pollen,"

Mrs Durham commends his "exquisite" coiffure, then admonishes, "Oh, don't brush it off, I like it on your dark hair." She wants to emasculate Maurice, just like Merchant and Ivory did – and just as critics over the years have emasculated Forster. (Leavitt 2005, xiv)

Leavitt loses critical perspective in defending the novel against the Merchant Ivory film, presented as a violation – an emasculation – of Forster. While not an insignificant detail, Maurice's follicular revision seems rather thin evidence of aesthetic failure. Leavitt pontificates from the hoary perspective that absolute fidelity to the source material is the only way to create a successful movie. Merchant Ivory get it coming and going – their work often gets criticized, as we have discussed, for being too faithful.

Ivory's transmogrification of Maurice's appearance responds to the adaptation-specific problem of visualizing literary dynamics. Which is to say, Ivory cinematically comments on the novel's interest in contrasting masculine styles, themselves commentaries on the distinct approaches to love, sex, and desire taken by each of the principal male characters.

Blond Maurice, imbued with the cultural signifiers of this hue, arguably signals the ordinariness, bluffness, typicality of the character as Forster envisioned him even more acutely than before. Moreover, as I have noted, by making him blond, Ivory links Forster's concept to Melville's Handsome Sailor, the ever-blond Billy Budd, offering a genealogy of queer desire in which his film version assumes a key part.

Back to Miller. As has been widely discussed, James Ivory has publicly bemoaned the fact that Guadagnino's film did not feature the male full-frontal nudity that Ivory incorporated into his screenplay and was less explicit in its male-male sex scenes. Ivory has pointed out in interviews and in his 2021 memoir *Solid Ivory* that he insisted on showing his actors naturalistically undressed in postcoital scenes (specifically the one in the hotel room after Maurice and Alec have shared a second time, after their tense meeting that leads them to the British Museum). Miller's critique cannot make room for Ivory's dissent from Guadagnino's filmmaking practice or for the latter's aesthetic choices because both artists, in the critic's view, remain hopelessly stuck in that self-hating, self-defeating MGM amber.

In a far more nuanced assessment, Rosalind Galt and Karl Schoonover focus on *Call Me by Your Name*'s Italian setting and the fact that Guadagnino changed the temporal setting of Aciman's novel from 1987 to 1983. The film "places its protagonists in a particular moment in the social, sexual, and political history of Italy, but it does so not to transport its viewers seamlessly into the past. Rather, the film's silent but overt narration makes the audience see the past through the lens of what is about to come next. In other words, the film never lets us forget the fragility of this moment, its finality, and the impossibility of its return. The Italy that we see is haunted by a future that will come to destroy it"[3] (Galt and Schoonover 2019, 12). These critics' analysis sheds light on Ivory's filmmaking in *Maurice*, which in turn sheds light on Forster's own moment and his efforts to tell a gay love story before the emergence of an unimaginable global disaster. Just as Forster's lovers ignite and fulfill their passions on the brink of the First World War, the lovers of Guadagnino's film share passions that will soon be under far greater social and personal threat during the first AIDS decade.

As I have striven to convey, I believe that Ivory's film, like Forster's novel before it, radically supports the idea that desire is politically as well as emotionally and spiritually transformative. Neither work may support this idea in ways that accord with queer theory at its white-hot political zenith, but queer radicalism exists on a spectrum as well. A film like *Maurice* would never have affected as many viewers as it has were its ambitions, effects, and resonance locked into an ideological program of stifling gay desire. Instead, the film reflects the impact desire makes on the subject who traces the impact's source and finds replenishment from it.

Merchant Ivory films are finally getting their due, appreciated as probing and full-bodied explorations of class and culture, sex and the body. Far from being hidebound, static statements, films such as *The Bostonians, A Room with*

a View, *Maurice*, and *Howards End* embrace the contradictions and the plen-
itude, the pricks and the tugs, the failures and the yearnings of their subjects
and narratives. Undeniably, my sense that *Maurice* is their finest achievement
is inextricable from its gay-male-love story content, but my hope is that this
volume has illuminated the sources of the film's strengths, its continuing
power to articulate a resonant personal vision that ignites our responses, its
lasting significance as a work that unapologetically and movingly put gay love
and desire onscreen.

Figure 40
Desire between men onscreen.

Notes

Chapter One

1 Ivory makes these remarks in the featurette "James Ivory and Pierre Lhomme on the Making of *Maurice*," Cohen Media Blu-ray of *Maurice* (2017).

2 Writing for the AV *Club*, Mike D'Angelo observes, "At some point during the 1990s, the term 'Merchant Ivory' – referring to films made by the team of producer Ismail Merchant and director James Ivory, usually in collaboration with screenwriter Ruth Prawer Jhabvala – became the cinematic equivalent of 'Masterpiece Theatre.' It signified quality, but often in a pejorative way, suggesting something British and tasteful and stuffy and frightfully dull" (D'Angelo 2015).

3 All biographical data on Ivory, Merchant, and Jhabvala is taken from Robert Emmet Long's invaluable study *The Films of Merchant Ivory*.

4 Monk problematizes the presumed centrality of Higson's role in the critical project of interrogating heritage cinema. "The contours of heritage-film criticism cannot accurately be credited to a single author. Essentially similar arguments had already been presented in academic articles by Tana Wollen (1991) and Cairns Craig (1991); but the anti-heritage-film discourse emerged over a period of years from multiple origins – journalistic first, academic later" (Monk 2002, 178).

5 I am saying "gay and lesbian" rather than LGBTQ+ because I believe it is more fitting for the moment of *Maurice*'s production and release.

6 Nissen refers to the reformer Eliza B. Duffey, author of the 1876 treatise *The Relations of the Sexes*.

7 Later a chapter in her book *Epistemology of the Closet*.

8 James, *The Bostonians*, 434.

9 This talkback is a featurette on the Cohen Media Group's 2019 Blu-ray of the restoration, "Conversations from the Quad: James Ivory on *The Bostonians*."

10 Laurence Raw argues, and I fully concur, that "Ivory should be recognized as one of the few contemporary filmmakers prepared to challenge accepted cinematic wisdom by producing innovative work that proposes more flexible social, psychological, and sexual relations, while simultaneously sustaining its appeal at the box-office. Perhaps this helps to explain why *The Bostonians* is such a moving and important intervention in the canon of Jamesian adaptations" (Raw 2006, 137).

11 Surprisingly, the perceptive film critic Vincent Canby was very harsh on this film in his *New York Times* review, calling it "a well-acted, literate but insufferably smug little movie that fictionalizes the life of Guy Burgess, who with Donald Maclean defected to Moscow in the early 1950s" (Canby 1984).

Chapter Two

1 All references will be from this edition and noted parenthetically in the main text.

2 Forster explains that he was once "encouraged to write an epilogue. It took the form of Kitty," one of Maurice's two sisters, "encountering two woodcutters some years later and gave universal dissatisfaction" to the many people who read the novel in draft form. His epilogue failed because his narrative ends in 1912 and the epilogue plunged it "into the

transformed England of the First World War." But that image of Maurice and Alec enduringly united and roaming the greenwood has become iconic, and Forster recognized the setting's importance. The novel, he writes, "belongs to an England where it was still possible to get lost. It belongs to the last moment of the greenwood," before the two world wars (Forster 2006, 254).

3 Discussing the crucial importance of Forster's inner circle and its on-going custom of exchanging work, Jodie Medd observes: "Given the ostensible contrast between Forster's literary prominence and his private queer life, Forster's truncated career writing publishable fiction may seem a casualty of heteronormativity, in which closeted queer writing and lives become public only in a posthumous future. This model of queer Bloomsbury is constituted by what was lost – a novelist's career – and what has been buried – the 'great unrecorded history' of male homosexuality, a history that Forster's own archive preserved, simultaneously remembering and anticipating 'a happier year.' In such absences, however, we may find something else. Forster's archive evidences a different kind of queer intervention, one in which the creation, appreciation and exchange of art between friends generate new possibilities of interpersonal intimacy, individual transformation and aesthetic experience, all central components of Bloomsbury's ethos" (Medd 2016, 259).

4 The Blu-ray includes deleted scenes of Risley's successful effort to die by suicide after being disgraced.

5 The chief hallmark, perhaps, of our contemporary sexual culture is that males are hyper-aware of being of sexual interest to other males and usually take great care to safeguard their bodies against invasive desiring gazes.

6 It is a pity, by the way, that the film eschews this darkly witty, wry, knowing Risley ultimately for its tragic, suicide-opting one. The latter feels like an inauthentic revision, whereas the former retains a resistant stance.

Chapter Three

1 See the chapters on *Maurice* in Long, *The Films of Merchant Ivory*, and Pym, *Merchant Ivory's English Landscape*, for background on the making of the film.

2 Critics also fault adaptations that deviate too much from their source material, providing ever more elaborate versions of "the book was better." Robin Wood, with his typically incisive impatience with such views, disputes the fidelity model that demands faithful screen adaptations. Wood elaborates his position in his BFI study of *The Wings of the Dove*, a film adaptation of Henry James's novel: "literature is literature, film is film. It's really as simple as that. There is no such thing as a faithful adaptation" (Wood 1999, 7–8). I share Wood's view while maintaining that we should pay attention to the myriad ways that a film adaptation interprets its source text.

3 Faithful adaptations find their antithesis in what the film adaptation-theorist Julie Grossman calls "hideous progeny": "Adaptations conceived as 'hideous progeny' change not only the way we view but also our ideas about what we are viewing. They 'destroy' other texts, even as they create new ones, revealing new perspectives on human identity and culture" (1).

4 In Classical Latin, V was pronounced like our W, and G was always hard. In Church Latin, V is pronounced like V, and G is soft before e, i, y, just like we're told it is in English. So *wa-ji-na*, Callow's pronunciation of "vagina," is incorrect, not because he does a soft G, but because he mixes the W from Classical Latin with the soft G from Church Latin. You'd expect a schoolmaster at a British school in the early twentieth century to use the Classical pronunciations, but if he did a consistently Church Latin pronunciation it would be odd but not

really wrong. And in the movie, when Ducie refers to the penis ("That … that *thing*"), he calls it a *membrum virilis*, rather than a *membrum virile*, using the masculine form of the adjective *virilis*, even though the noun membrum is neuter. That's an outright error, like saying *la beau fille* or *le belle garcon* would be in French. My thanks to Alexander Beecroft for the Latin analysis.

5 Those sunglasses are not anachronistic. In 1752, the optician and scientific inventor James Ayscough introduced proto-sunglasses, spectacles with lenses tinted blue or green.

6 We see an older man dutifully mopping each step. Domestic workers abound in the film; the topic of labour in Merchant Ivory demands a discrete study.

7 One thinks of the final, similar shot at the end of *Call Me by Your Name*, as heartbroken Elio stares into the fireplace in an eternity of loss after hearing from Oliver that he is getting married.

8 According to the actor's IMBD page, "A bisexual with many partners during his life, [Elliott] tested HIV positive in 1987 and was diagnosed with AIDS in 1988. He continued working until a year before he died in 1992. Following his death, some sources stated that he acquired the AIDS virus from a blood transfusion. However, his widow Susan documented their open marriage and her husband's bisexuality in her book *Denholm Elliott: Quest for Love*, published two years after his death." Accessed on 25 September 2021: https://m.imdb.com/name/nm0001186/trivia.

9 In the novel, in response to Clive's question, "Shared what?" Maurice explains, "All I have. Which includes my body" (243). Originally, this last exchange between Maurice and Clive was much longer and included more of Forster's dialogue. The exchange in its entirety can be found among the deleted scenes on the Cohen Media Blu-ray.

Chapter Four

1 Matthew Tinkcom's *Queer Theory and Brokeback Mountain* (London: Bloomsbury, 2017) debunks the clichés associated with *Brokeback Mountain* as the "gay cowboy movie" and emphasizes its significance as a class critique. Tinkcom is extremely attentive to issues of female experience, misogyny, and feminism, discussing the intersections between the latter and queer theory and the significance of the film's analysis of homophobia's impact on women and the non-white.

2 For a rebuttal to Miller's reading, see my chapter on *Rope* in Greven (2017).

3 See also Wallace (2020) for further discussions about Miller's views.

References

Ang, Raymond. 2022. "James Ivory Has Been Making Films for 70 Years. His Latest Might Be His Most Personal." *GQ*, 3 November 2022. https://www.gq.com/story/james-ivory-a-cooler-climate-profile/.

Ansen, David. 1987. "A Closet with a View." *Newsweek*, 21 September 1987.

Bergan, Ronald. 2012. "Richard Robbins obituary." *Guardian*, 13 November 2012. https://www.theguardian.com/film/2012/nov/13/richard-robbins.

Bieri, James. 2005. *Percy Bysshe Shelley: A Biography: Exile of Unfulfilled Reknown, 1816–1822*. Newark, DE: University of Delaware Press.

Bram, Christopher [Chris]. 1987. "An English Everyman: James Ivory and Ismail Merchant Talk about the Making of *Maurice*." *New York Native* 231, 21 September 1987.

British Film Institute. 2005. "Back to the Future: The Fall and Rise of the British Film Industry in the 1980s – An Information Briefing." https://www2.bfi.org.uk/sites/bfi.org.uk/files/downloads/bfi-back-to-the-future-the-fall-and-rise-of-the-british-film-industry-in-the-1980s.pdf.

Bronski, Michael. 1987. "Pretty Postures: Ivory and Merchant Put Out Forster's Fires in *Maurice*." *Gay Community News*, 25–31 October 1987.

Canby, Vincent. 1984. "Review of *Another Country*." *New York Times*, 29 June 1984. https://www.nytimes.com/1984/06/29/movies/the-screen-another-country.html.

Chee, Alexander. 2021. "The Afterlives of E.M. Forster." *New Republic*, 21 September 2021. https://newrepublic.com/article/163578/em-forster-after-lives-maurice-alec.

Crompton, Louis. 1985. *Byron and Greek Love: Homophobia in 19th Century England*. Berkeley: University of California Press.

D'Angelo, Mike. 2015. "Remember When Merchant Ivory Was a Brand to Believe In, Not an Insult?" *AV Club*, 30 August 2015. https://www.avclub.com/remember-when-merchant-ivory-was-a-brand-to-believe-in-1798185045.

Dyer, Richard. 2002. "Homosexuality and Heritage." In *The Culture of Queers*, 204–28. New York: Taylor and Francis Group.

– 2001. "Nice Young Men Who Sell Antiques: Gay Men in Heritage Cinema." In *Film/Literature/Heritage*, edited by Ginette Vincendeau, 43–8. London: British Film Institute.

Finch, Mark, and Richard Kwietniowski. 1988. "Melodrama and Maurice: Homo Is Where the HET Is." *Screen* 29, no. 3 (Summer): 72–83. https://doi.org/10.1093/screen/29.3.72.

Forster, E.M. 2006. *Maurice* (1971). New York: W.W. Norton & Co.

Freeman, Hadley. 2021. "James Ivory: 'I Keep Being Asked, Was It Difficult, Your Life? My Life, If Anything, Was Too Easy.'" *Guardian*, 29 October 2021. https://www.theguardian.com/film/2021/oct/29/james-ivory-i-keep-being-asked-was-it-difficult-your-life-my-life-if-anything-was-too-easy.

Fuller, Graham. 1987. "Keeping Faith with E.M. Forster." *Listener*, 22 October 1987.

Galt, Rosalind, and Karl Schoonover. 2019. "Untimely Desires, Historical Efflorescence, and Italy in *Call Me by Your Name*." *Italian Culture* 37, no.1: 64–81, https://www.tandfonline.com/doi/abs/10.1080/01614622.2019.1609220.

Gilbey, Ryan. 2018. "Interview: James Ivory: Why Ismail Merchant and I Kept Our Love Secret." *Guardian*, 27 March 2018. https://www.theguardian.com/film/2018/mar/27/james-ivory-ismail-merchant-love-secret-call-me-by-your-name-nudity.

Goldstein, Gary. 2017. "James Ivory and James Wilby Look Back at the Making of *Maurice*, a Time When Gay Happy Endings Were Rare." *Los Angeles Times*, 30 May 2017. https://www.latimes.com/entertainment/movies/la-et-mn-maurice-feature-20170529-story.html.

Greven, David. 2017. *Intimate Violence: Hitchcock, Sex, and Queer Theory*. New York: Oxford University Press.

– 2018. "Unlovely Spectacle: D.A. Miller on *Call Me by Your Name*." *Film International*, 13 March 2018. http://filmint.nu/?p=23937.

Hachem, Samir. 1987. "Inside Maurice: Actor James Wilby on Playing the Dark Side of a Gay Romantic Here." *Advocate*, 8 December 1987.

Halleck, Mark. 1987. "Review of *Maurice*." *New York Native*, 21 September 1987.

Hart, Kylo-Patrick R., ed. 2006. *Film and Sexual Politics*. United Kingdom: Cambridge Scholars Publisher.

Harvey, Stephen. 1987. "Men in Love." *Village Voice*, 22 September 1987.

Higson, Andrew, ed. 1997a. *Dissolving Views: Key Writings on British Cinema*. London: Bloomsbury Publishing Plc.

– 1997b. "The Heritage Film and British Cinema." In *Dissolving Views: Key Writings on British Cinema*, edited by Andrew Higson, 232–48.

– 2006. "Re-presenting the National Past: Nostalgia and Pastiche in the Heritage Film" (1993). In *Fires Were Started: British Cinema and Thatcherism*, 2nd edition, edited by Lester Friedman, 91–109. London: Wallflower.

Hollinghurst, Alan. 1987. "Suppressive Nostalgia." *Times Literary Supplement*, 6 November 1987.

Houlbrook, Matt. 2005. *Queer London: Perils and Pleasures in the Sexual Metropolis, 1918–1957*. Chicago Series on Sexuality, History, and Society. Chicago: University of Chicago Press.

Ingersoll, Earl G. 2012. *Filming Forster: The Challenges of Adapting E.M. Forster's Novels for the Screen*. Fairleigh Dickinson University Press.

Ivory, James, and Peter Cameron (editor). 2021. *Solid Ivory: Memoirs*. New York: Farrar, Straus and Giroux.

Ivory, James, and Robert Emmet Long. 2005. *James Ivory in Conversation: How Merchant Ivory Makes Its Movies*. Berkeley, CA: University of California Press.

James, Henry. 2009. *The Bostonians* (1886). New York: Oxford University Press.

Jasanoff, Maya. 2018. "Ruth Prawer Jhabvala and the Art of Ambivalence." *New Yorker*, 31 December 2018. https://www.newyorker.com/magazine/2019/01/07/ruth-prawer-jhabvala-and-the-art-of-ambivalence.

Kael, Pauline. 1989. *Hooked*. New York: Dutton.

Leavitt, David. 2005. "Introduction." In *Maurice*, xi–xxxvi. London: Penguin Classics.

Lodge, Guy. 2017. "*Maurice* at 30: The Gay Period Drama the World Wasn't Ready For." *Guardian*, 19 May 2017. https://www.theguardian.com/film/2017/may/19/maurice-film-period-drama-merchant-ivory.

Long, Robert Emmet. 1997. *The Films of Merchant Ivory*. Newly Updated ed. New York: Abrams.

– 2006. *James Ivory in Conversation: How Merchant Ivory Makes Its Movies*. Berkeley, CA: The University of California Press.

Marks, Martin. 2001. "Robbins, Richard." *Grove Music Online*. https://www.oxfordmusiconline.com/grovemusic/view/10.1093/gmo/9781561592630.001.0001/omo-9781561592630-e-0000051330.

Maslin, Janet. 1987. "Film: *Maurice* in Style of Ivory and Merchant." *New York Times*, 18 September 1987.

Medd, Jodie. 2016. "'I Didn't Know There Could Be Such Writing': The Aesthetic Intimacy of E.M. Forster and T.E. Lawrence." In *Queer Bloomsbury*, edited by Helt Brenda and Detloff Madelyn, 258–75. Edinburgh: Edinburgh University Press.

Miller, D.A. 1990. "Anal Rope." *Representations* 32 (Fall): 114–33.

— 2021. "Elio's Education." *Los Angeles Review of Books*, 19 February 2018. https://lareviewofbooks.org/article/elios-education.

Mitchell, Mark, and David Leavitt, eds. 1999. *Pages Passed from Hand to Hand: The Hidden Tradition of Homosexual Literature in English from 1748 to 1914*. London: Vintage.

Moffat, Wendy. 2010. *A Great Unrecorded History: A New Life of E.M. Forster*. New York: Farrar, Straus & Giroux.

Monk, Claire. 1995. "The British 'Heritage Film' and Its Critics." *Critical Survey* 7, no. 2: 116–24.

— 2020. "*Maurice* without Ending: From Forster's Palimpsest to Fan-Text." In *Twenty-First-Century Readings of E.M. Forster's "Maurice."* Liverpool English Texts and Studies 83, edited by E. Sutton and T.-H. Tsai. Liverpool: Liverpool University Press.

— 2021. "The British Heritage-Film Debate Revisited." In *British Historical Cinema*, edited by Claire Monk and Amy Sargeant, 176–98.

Monk, Claire, and Amy Sargeant. 2002a. *British Historical Cinema*. London: Taylor & Francis Group.

— 2002b. "Introduction: The Past in British Cinema." In *British Historical Cinema*, edited by Claire Monk and Amy Sargeant, 1–14.

Nehme, Farran Smith. 2016. "*A Room with a View* (1985)." *Film Comment*, 17 February 2016. https://www.filmcomment.com/blog/on-a-room-with-a-view-1985/.

Nissen, Axel. 2009. *Manly Love: Romantic Friendship in American Fiction*. Chicago: University of Chicago Press.

Ozick, Cynthia. 1971. "Forster as Homosexual." *Commentary*.

Pally, Marcia. 1987. "*Maurice*: A Perfect Fantasy." *Advocate*, 15 September 1987.

Patriche, Alina. 2006. "Rooms with Different Views: Restoring Gay Images to the Past in Contemporary Costume Film." In *Film and Sexual Politics: A Critical Reader*, edited by Kylo Patrick Hart, 217–29. Cambridge, UK: Cambridge Scholars Press.

Perry, George. 1987. "Review of *Maurice*." *Sunday Times* (London), 8 November 1987.

Piggford, George. 2016. "Camp Sites: Forster and the Biographies of Queer Bloomsbury." In *Queer Bloomsbury*, edited by Helt Brenda and Detloff Madelyn, 64–88. Edinburgh: Edinburgh University Press.

Pym, John. 1995. *Merchant Ivory's English Landscape*. London: H.N. Abrams, Publishers.

Raw, Laurence. 2006. *Adapting Henry James to the Screen: Gender, Fiction, and Film*. Lanham, MD: Scarecrow Press.

Rayside, David M. 1992. "Homophobia, Class and Party in England." *Canadian Journal of Political Science / Revue canadienne de science politique* 25, no. 1 (March): 121–49.

Rowe, John Carlos. 1998. *The Other Henry James*. Durham, NC: Duke University Press.

Sedgwick, Eve Kosofsky. 1990. "The Beast in the Closet: James and the Writing of Homosexual Panic." *Epistemology of the Closet*, 182–212. Berkeley, CA: University of California Press.

Sen, Mayukh. 2019. "The Queer Appetites of Ismail Merchant." *Hazlitt*, 6 August 2019. https://hazlitt.net/longreads/queer-appetites-ismail-merchant.

Singh, Avtar. 1996. *The Novels of E.M. Forster*. Atlantic Publishers & Distributors (P) Limited.

Speidel, Suzanne. 2014. "'Scenes of Marvellous Variety': The Work-in-Progress Screenplays of *Maurice*." *Journal of Adaptation in Film and Performance* 7, no. 3: 299–318.

Strauss, Neil. 1996. "Lush Odes to the Art of Two Film Makers." *New York Times*, 19 September 1996.

Thomas, Kevin. 1987. "*Maurice*: A Homosexual's Odyssey." *Los Angeles Times*, 1 October 1987.

Vidal, Belén. 2012a. *Heritage Film: Nation, Genre and Representation*. London: Wallflower Press.

— 2012b. *Figuring the Past: Period Film and the Mannerist Aesthetic.* Amsterdam University Press.

Wallace, Lee. 2020. *Reattachment Theory: Queer Cinema of Remarriage.* Durham, NC: Duke University Press.

Walters, Margaret. 1987. "Cinema." *Listener* 118, no. 3036 (5 November 1987).

Waugh, Thomas. 2000. *The Fruit Machine: Twenty Years of Writings on Queer Cinema.* Durham, NC: Duke University Press.

Williams, Michael. 2018. *Film Stardom and the Ancient Past: Idols, Artefacts and Epics.* United Kingdom: Palgrave Macmillan UK.

Wood, Robin. 1999. *The Wings of the Dove: Henry James in the 1990s.* BFI Modern Classics. London: British Film Institute.

Worthen, John. 2019. *The Life of Percy Bysshe Shelley: A Critical Biography.* Hoboken, NJ: Wiley Blackwell.

Index